IN FEW WORDS

EN POCAS
PALABRAS

IN FEW WORDS

EN POCAS PALABRAS

A Compendium of ◨ LATINO ◨ Folk Wit and Wisdom

A BILINGUAL COLLECTION BY

José Antonio Burciaga

Edited by Carol & Thomas Christensen

MERCURY HOUSE

SAN FRANCISCO

Published in the United States of America by Mercury House, San Francisco, California, a nonprofit publishing company devoted to the free exchange of ideas and guided by a dedication to literary values.

United States Constitution, First Amendment: Congress shall make no law respecting an establishment of religion, or prohibiting the free exercise thereof; or abridging the freedom of speech, or of the press; or the right of the people peaceably to assemble, and to petition the Government for a redress of grievances.

Printed on recycled, acid-free paper and manufactured in the United States of America.

Translation of author's preface into Spanish © Graciela López Díaz.

Editors' thanks to participants in the "Dichos Round Table"—Thomas Appèl-Braun, Po Bronson, Claire Christensen, Kirsten Edmondson, Dolores Jalbert, Kirsten Janene-Nelson, Karyn Johnson, Josh Kornbluth, and Sara Soto—who assisted with some of the translations. Thanks too to Catherine Park, Dolores Jalbert, Anh Tuan Pham, and Alison Satake for grueling work on the index and other editorial help. Production editing by Kirsten Janene-Nelson.

Designed by Thomas Christensen in Adobe Bulmer.

Library of Congress Cataloguing-in-Publication Data:
Burciaga, José Antonio.
   En pocas palabras = In few words : a compendium of Latino folk wit and wisdom : a bilingual collection / by José Antonio Burciaga; edited by Carol and Thomas Christensen.
       p.   cm.
Includes bibliographical references (p. 255) and index.
   ISBN 1-56279-093-5 (alk. paper)
   1. Proverbs, Spanish. 2. Proverbs, Spanish—Translations into English. 3. Proverbs, Mexican. I. Christensen, Carol, 1947– II. Christensen, Thomas, 1948– III. Title.
PN6491.B87   1996
398.9´61–DC20   96-29427
                                                CIP

9 8 7 6 5 4 3 2 1
FIRST EDITION

Contents
Contenido

Con todo mi cariño,
dedico esta colección
a las mujeres de mi vida:
mi madre María Guadalupe Fernández de Burciaga
mi segunda madre Rebeca Jiménez de Preciado
mi querida compañera y esposa Cecilia María Preciado Burciaga
mi querida hija María Rebeca Burciaga

I thank and acknowledge the following friends
for their contributions:
Victoria Díaz
Rolando Villalobos
Charlie Ericksen
Stanford University Library
Other Inspiring Collectors noted in the Bibliography

Prólogo

por
José
Antonio
Burciaga

Los proverbios tienen un rol importante en la cultura, sociedad y educación de la gente en el mundo entero. Son comunes especialmente en los países en donde se habla español debido a su fuerte tradición oral. De España hasta Mesoamérica, de la Antigua, Arabia y las influencias judías hasta los indígenas mexicanos, estos dichos siguen manteniendo su belleza metafórica en el uso natural.

Las frases populares son conocidas como dichos que no es lo mismo que los proverbios, estos últimos contienen un pensamiento filosófico más extenso. En español, los dichos son utilizados en una conversación para explicar o descibir una situación, una palabra, o un sujeto.

Los dichos son frases como:

> Terco como una mula.
> *Stubborn as a mule.*

O bien pueden ser refranes, los cuales se sobre entienden, como por ejemplo,

> El perro que no sale no encuentra hueso.
> *A dog that doesn't go outside finds no bones.*

Entre las primeras generaciones latinas en los Estados Unidos, los dichos normalmente hacen renacer recuerdos dormidos. Cuando visitamos a nuestros parientes, ya sea en Nuevo México, Texas, Puerto Rico, o cualquier otro país como México, Guatemala, Argentina o España, nuestros parientes, abuelos, tías y tíos están llenos de proverbios, palabras de amor, cuidado y advertencias, palabras de sabios consejos y sabiduría.

> Dichos de los viejitos son evangelios chiquitos.
> *The sayings of our elders should be taken as gospel.*

Proverbs have an important role in the culture, socialization, and education of people around the world. They are especially popular in Spanish-speaking countries, which have a strong oral tradition. From Spain to Mesoamérica, from ancient Arabic and Jewish influences to those of the indigenous Mexican peoples, these sayings maintain their metaphorical beauty in the use of nature.

Spanish popular sayings are known as *dichos*. These are not the same as *proverbios*, which are more extensive philosophical thoughts. In Spanish, dichos may be used in a conversation to explain or describe a situation, a word, or a subject.

Dichos may be phrases, such as:

> Terco como una mula.
> *Stubborn as a mule.*

Or they may be *refranes*, popular sayings that can stand alone, for example, this piece of advice:

> El perro que no sale no encuentra hueso.
> *A dog that doesn't go outside finds no bones.*

Among first-generation Latinos in the United States, dichos often reawaken dormant memories. When we visited our relatives—whether in New Mexico, Texas, Puerto Rico, or any mother country from Mexico, Guatemala, Argentina, to Spain—our relatives, *abuelos, tíos,* and *tías,* were filled with proverbs, words of love, caution, and admonition, words of sage advice and wisdom.

> Dichos de los viejitos son evangelios chiquitos.
> *The sayings of our elders should be taken as gospel.*

Prólogo

Los proverbios nos hacen recordar el tiempo en que una simple conversación creaba arte. Decir y mantener un pensamiento positivo con un tono firme de voz en donde nuestros antiguos mensajes fueron leccions de moralidad, reglas de etiqueta y conducta. Son tan simples y al mismo tiempo tan ciertas que fluyen fácilmente en las conversaciones familiares, entre chismes y nuevas. Los dichos acentúan, enfatizan, afirman o refutan un punto. Se les veía de cierta manera como puntos claves para protegerse de la sociedad y de sus reglas sociales para con los niños.

Hemos dejado que estos dichos vayan de oído en oído, pero eventualmente regresan a uno, recapturados en el eco de la memoria, a medida que vamos creciendo y emulando la sabiduría de nuestros antepasados. Y así continuan generación tras generación, por lo menos hasta que aprendemos una nueva lengua. Despúes corremos el riesgo de perder o transculturizar estas palabras de sabiduría, al mismo tiempo aparecen nuevos dichos entre ese cruce de polinizacións con los angloamericanos.

Mientras tanto los dichos siguen siendo una ventana al pasado para cualquier sociedad ya sea rural del campo así como para las pequeñas comunidades. Estos proverbios normalmente de ciertas regiones, nos enseñan mucho sobre la cultura española-mexicana y la de los indígenas y otras culturas latinoamericanas. A algunos dichos se les reconoce su antiguedad por las palabras utilizadas o por sus referencias implícitas hacia los animales o bestias de carga, como lo son los bueyes y las mulas.

Nuevo México es una mina de oro en cuanto a dichos en español se refiere. Gracias al aislamiento e incomunicación

Such proverbs are a reminder of a time when conversation was an easy art form. Uttered in a firm but thoughtful tone of voice, our elders' messages were lessons in morals, rules of etiquette, and conduct. These simple but sincere truths flowed easily in family conversations, around gossip or news items. Dichos punctuated, emphasized, affirmed, or refuted a point. They were social guard rails and rules of thumb for children.

We may have let these dichos go in one ear and out the other, but eventually they come back to us, recaptured in the echo of a memory, as we grow older and emulate the wisdom of our elders. And so it continues, as we pass them along from generation to generation. At least until we learn a new language. Then we run the risk of losing or transculturating these words of wisdom—at the same time that new sayings sprout from this cross-pollination with Anglo America.

Still, dichos allow us a window into the past, when much of the world's population lived in rural agrarian societies and smaller communities. These proverbs—often regional in nature—teach us much about Spanish, Mexican, indigenous, and other Latin American cultures. Some dichos show their antiquity by the words used or the untold references to animals as beasts of burden, for example, oxen and mules.

New Mexico is a goldmine of ancient Spanish dichos. Because of its centuries-old isolation, many fifteenth-century Spanish words, names, tools, social and religious practices are still alive there.

One young woman in New Mexico asked her parents

que tuvo por siglos, muchas palabras del siglo XV, nombres, utencilios y prácticas religiosas sociales siguen vigentes. En alguna ocasión una joven mujer en Nuevo México les preguntó a sus padres y abuela que le dijeran algunos dichos, en ese momento no pudieron decirle ninguno, pero tan pronto comenzaron a platicar, los dichos empezaron a fluirsin el menor esfuerzo. Los dichos son una parte escencial de cuaquier conversasión, ni siquiera se mencionan como citando alguna frase o entre comillándolas.

Así mismo en las culturas latinas al corregir o enmendar algo es mejor si se hace con cierta gracia o indirectamente. De ahí la popularidad de los dichos con ese maravilloso estilo y manera de enseñar: brindan de alguna manera pronunciamientos, ediciones, juicios o bien afirman las verdades culturales que son evidentes, así como principios fundamentales y reglas de conducta. Los dichos represetan la corriente popular de sabiduría en la vida diaria de la gente. Pretenden crear un lazo común de entendimiento y respeto en la sociedad.

Los dichos nos recuerdan que en tiempos pasados antes de que las escuelas aparecieran los niños eran educados en la propia casa con proverbios. Por eso la Biblia tiene su "libro de proverbios," pero no todos los dichos son verdades biblícas, algunos son adjudicados al diablo, racismo o bien a las ciertas posturas ignorantes algunas han sido parte de un determinado valor social en el pasado y que en estos días son obsoletos.

Mestizo educado, diablo colorado.
An educated mestizo turns into a red devil.

Muchos dichos referentes al sexo relegan a la mujer a

and grandmother for some dichos. They couldn't think of any. But as soon as they began conversing, the dichos started to flow—effortlessly. Dichos are an essential part of any conversation, not separate entities set off in quotation marks.

In Latino cultures, correcting or redressing someone is best accomplished with empathy or indirection. Thus the popularity of dichos, with their wonderful style and manner of teaching: they offer a way to make pronouncments, edicts, and judgments, to affirm the culture's self-evident truths, fundamental principles, and rules of conduct. Dichos represent the popular mainstream wisdom of the common people in their daily lives. They seek to form a common bond of mutual understanding and respect in society.

Dichos remind us that long before schools were invented, children were taught at home with proverbs. Thus the Bible has its "Book of Proverbs." But not all dichos are the bible truth. Some were authored by evil, racist, or ignorant attitudes and some were at one time part of ancient social values, now obsolete:

> Mestizo educado, diablo colorado.
> *An educated mestizo turns into a red devil.*

Many sexist dichos relegated women to an inferior social position. The Hispanic, Arabic, and Aztec cultural histories are notorious in this respect. Many dichos equated poverty with laziness. For the most part, such proverbs are not included in this collection. Why repeat them in this day and age?

una postura inferior dentro de la sociedad, sobre todo en las culturas hispanas, árabes y aztecas. Muchos otros dichos igualan o relacionan a la pobreza con la pereza. La mayoría de este tipo de dichos no están incluídos en esta colección. ¿Porque repetirlos en esta época y en nuestros días?

El que anda por malos caminos, levanta malos polvos.
If you go down a dirty road, you'll raise a filthy dust.

Esta colección no ha sido proyectada para ser una completa e histórica variedad de dichos, se han querido incluir los proverbios que siguen teniendo válidez y uso hoy día. Incluyendo dichos que han tendido vida dentro de la literatura, por ejemplo, en *Don Quijote* de Miguel de Cervantes o en Shakespeare.

Algunos de los dichos aquí mencionados están más llenos de ingenio que de sabiduría. También muchos tienen varias interpretaciones y pueden ser utilizados en más de una situación, lo que los hace clasificarse más en el campo de arte que en el de la ciencia.

Muchos dichos son difíciles de traducir. Los albures, por ejemplo, so proverbios maliciosos que hacen alusiones a mensajes de doble sentido, la cual implica otro significado, normalmente referidos al sexo. En México, estos albures, son parte de una subcultura picaresca. Estos juegos de palabras requieren de cierto conocimiento y destreza en el uso de palabras y términos.

Los Dichos no pertenecen a nigun género específico. Mientras en inglés debemos escoger para el masculino "his," y para el femenino "her," y el "their" para referirse al "su" de ellos/ellas, en español sólo usamos el posesivo "su" para referirnos a él, ella, o su de ellos/ellas, sin más dificul-

El que anda por malos caminos, levanta malos polvos.
If you go down a dirty road, you'll raise a filthy dust.

This collection was not intended to be a complete, historical, and unabridged assortment of dichos. It is intended to include many proverbs that are still valid and useful today. It includes some dichos that either come from literature or live on in it, for example, in Miguel Cervantes's *Don Quixote* or in Shakespeare.

Some of the dichos collected here offer more wit than wisdom. Many dichos have several interpretations and can be used in more than one situation, which makes classifying them more of an art than a science.

Many dichos pose difficulties for the translator. *Albures,* for example, are malicious proverbs that make allusions to a secondary message, a double meaning, often sexist in nature. In Mexico, they are part of a picaresque subculture. These word games require a knowledge and dexterous use of words and terms.

Often dichos are not gender specific. While in English one is forced to choose among the masculine *to each his own,* the feminine *to each her own,* the wordy and awkward *to each his or her own,* and the ungrammatical *to each their own,* the Spanish possessive *su* (his/her/their) presents no such difficulty. Reluctantly, I have chosen to convey at least something of the craft and concision of the dichos, at the cost of introducing gender: *To each his own.*

Most dichos are poetic and rhythmic in nature. In translation, they may lose their rhyme, but not their reason.

Prólogo

tad. Sin mucho entusiasmo, he convenido transmitir de manera concisa por lo menos algo sobre el oficio de hacer dichos, aún a costa de presentar el género de cada uno.

La mayoría de los dichos son poéticos y de ritmo natural. Al traducirlos seguramente perderan su ritmo pero no su sentido.

Disfrutenlos, estoy seguro que muchos sonarán como eco a las palabras de sus padres y abuelos, al mismo tiempo reafirmarán sus creencias.

> En tus apuros y afanes,
> escucha los consejos de refranes.
> *When you're broke and feeling blue,*
> *let proverbs tell you what to do.*

Enjoy them! Many will echo your parents' or grand-parents' words. They may reaffirm your beliefs.

En tus apuros y afanes,
escucha los consejos de refranes.
When you're broke and feeling blue,
let proverbs tell you what to do.

Preface

IN FEW WORDS

EN POCAS
PALABRAS

Beginning
Principio

Dios es Principio.
God is the Beginning.

Lo que bien empieza bien termina.
What begins well ends well.

Buen principio, la mitad es hecho.
Well begun is half done.

*Principio
quieren
las cosas.*

Everything
needs a
beginning.

ANIMALS

LOS ANIMALES

Cuiden sus gallinas, que mi coyote anda suelto.
Take care of your hens, my coyote is loose.

El que es buen gallo, donde quiera canta.
A good rooster sings anywhere.

La música ablanda a las fieras.
Music soothes the savage beast.

Al perro más flaco se le cargan más las pulgas.
The skinniest dog will carry the most fleas.

La cochina más flaca es la que quiebra el chiquero.
The scrawniest pig is the one that breaks the pigpen.
(The least likely can cause the most problems.)

Tirar al león.
Throw it to the lion.
(To care less.)

Animals
Animales

Perro con maña aunque le quemen el hocico.

A dog with the same bad habit even if they burn its nose.

La zorra mudará los dientes pero no las mientes.
The fox's teeth may fall away but her wiles are here to stay.

La cabra siempre tira al monte.
The goat always heads for the mountain.
(*We are victims of our habits.*)

Gallina que come huevos, aunque le quemen el pico.
A hen that eats eggs even if they burn her beak.

Si hubiera sido animal te pica.
If it had been an animal it would have bitten you.

Matar pulgas a balazos.
To kill fleas with bullets.

Con dinero baila el perro.
Finance will make the dog dance.

Nunca sabe el cazador donde le sale la liebre.
The hunter never knows where the rabbit will appear.

De lo contado, come el lobo.
The wolf eats where it may.

Camarón que duerme se lo lleva la corriente.
Shrimp that sleep are swept away by the current.

Entrar como burro sin mecate.
To walk in like a loose donkey.

Animals
Animales

A cada guajolote le llega su Nochebuena.
Every turkey has its Christmas Eve.
(*Every dog has his day.*)

Cree el león que todos son de su condición.
The lion thinks everyone else is the same as he is.

El gallo más grande es el que más recio canta.
The biggest rooster sings the loudest.

Cada gallo canta en su corral; pero el mexicano,
que es muy bueno, canta en el suyo y en el ajeno.
*Every cock crows in its own corral; but the Mexican cock is
especially good: It crows in both its own and its neighbor's.*

Estar como perro en barrio ajeno.
To be like a dog in a strange neighborhood.

Quien quiere a Romero, quiere a su perro.
Who loves Romero, loves his dog.
(*Love me, love my dog.*)

Cada uno tiene su modo de matar pulgas.
Everyone has his own way of killing fleas.

Como perro mojado, curtido y avergonzado.
Like a dog, wet, weathered, and shamefaced.

Cuando el perro es bravo, hasta los de la casa muerde.
A fierce dog will bite even its master.

A cada puerco le llega su San Martín.

Every pig has a saint's day.

(Every dog has its day.)

Animals
Animales

De noche todos
los gatos son
pardos.

All cats are
gray in the
night.

Muerta es la abeja que daba la miel y la cera.
Dead is the bee that made the honey and the wax.
(The golden goose is dead.)

No hay gavilán gordo ni coyote barrigón.
There is no fat hawk nor fat-bellied coyote.

Si no es gato, es gata, y si no gatito.
If it's not a male cat, it's a female cat; if not, it's a kitten.

Más vale ser cabeza de ratón que cola de león.
Better to be a mouse's head than a lion's tail.

No es tan bravo el león como lo pintan.
The lion is not as bad as we paint him.

Para gato viejo, ratón tierno.
For an old cat, a tender mouse.

Dos gatos en un costal, no juntos pueden estar.
Two cats in a sack can't be together.

Cuando el gato no está en casa, los ratones se pasean.
When the cat's away, the mice will play.

El mejor caballo necesita espuelas.
The best horse needs spurs.

Caballo corredor no necesita espuelas.
A running horse does not need spurs.

Animals
Animales

Caballo que vuela, no quiere espuela.
A horse that soars doesn't need spurs.

No confundir los animales de pelo con los de pluma.
Do not confuse animals of fur with those of feathers.

Caballo de rico, rico caballo.
Horse of a rich owner, rich horse.

Al ojo del amo engorda el caballo.
The horse grows fat in the eyes of its master.

Más vale perro de rico y no santo de pobre.
Better the life of a rich dog than that of a poor saint.

El perro del hortelano, que ni come ni deja comer.
*The orchard keeper's dog can't eat, and it won't
allow others to eat.*

Gane mi gallo y aunque sea rabón.
May my rooster win, even without a tail.

Desde lejos se conoce el pájaro que es calandria.
From afar one can distinguish a bird that is a lark.

Por el canto se conoce al pájaro.
A bird is known by its song.

Más vale pájaro en mano que cien volando.
A bird in hand is worth two in the bush.

*Ese perro no
me muerde
otra vez.*

That dog won't
bite me
again.

(I won't make
that same
mistake
again.)

GOOD WORDS

LAS BUENAS PALABRAS

La cultura cura la locura.
Culture cures craziness.

Hablando se entiende la gente.
People learn by talking.

¿Con esa boca comes?
You can eat with that mouth?
(*To someone who uses coarse language.*)

El que no duda, no sabe cosa alguna.
If you never have a doubt, you can't know what things are about.
(*If you don't ask questions, you won't understand anything.*)

Para saber hablar, hay que saber escuchar.
To know how to talk, you have to know how to listen.

Los locos y los refranes nos dicen las cosas reales.
Fools and proverbs tell us the truth.

Quien no oye consejo, no llega a viejo.
A person who won't take advice won't live long enough to give any.

Los sabios componen dichos y los tontos los repiten.
The wise compose proverbs and the foolish repeat them.

Bueno aconsejar, mejor remediar.
It's okay to give advice about problems, but it's better to solve them.

El mal ajeno da consejo.
Other people's problems offer the best advice.

El consejo no es bien recibido, donde no es pedido.
Advice not sought will always be fought.

El que habla del camino es porque lo tiene andado.
I can talk about that road because I've walked it.
(Speaking from experience.)

Los consejos no pedidos los dan los entremetidos.
If nobody asked for advice, it's meddling to give it.

De la necesidad nace el consejo.
Need breeds proverbs.
(Necessity is the mother of suggestions.)

Advice
Consejo

A buen entendedor, pocas palabras bastan.

For a good listener, a few words will do.

Advice
Consejo

*La cantidad de
consejos siempre
es más que la
demanda.*

There's always
more advice
than there is
demand
for it.

Del viejo, al consejo.
From the old, old saws.

Dichos de los viejitos son evangelios chiquitos.
The sayings of our elders should be taken as gospel.

El consejo es más facil de dar que tomar.
Advice is easier to give than to follow.

Persona refranera, medida y certera.
An old saw-sayer, safe and sure.

Para dar consejos, todos; para tomarlos, pocos.
Everybody likes to give advice, few like to take it.

La persona no ha de ser de dichos sino de hechos.
A person should not be made out of talk but of deeds.

Del dicho al hecho hay mucho trecho.
It's a long way from the word to the deed.

Dichos no rompen panzas pero adolecen almas.
Sayings don't rip bellies, they rend souls.

En tus apuros y afanes, escucha los
consejos de refranes.
*When you're broke and feeling blue,
let proverbs tell you what to do.*

La palabra vale lo que vale el que la dice.
A word is as good as the person who gives it.

La persona honrada, de su palabra es siempre esclava.
People of honor are always slave to their words.

Más hiere mala palabra que espada afilada.
A harsh word cuts deeper than a sharp sword.

No hay palabra mal dicha que no sea mal tomada.
Any word that's badly spoken will be badly taken.

Por tus propias palabras serás juzgado.
By your own words you shall be condemned.
   —New Testament, Matthew, XII, 37

Palabras sin obras, guitarras sin cuerdas.
Words without deeds are like guitars without strings.

La rana más aplastada es la que más recio grita.
The flattest frog croaks the loudest.

Día nubloso, poco lluvioso.
Clouds frightening, little lightning.
(Great talker, no action.)

Al buey por el cuerno y al hombre con la palabra.
Take the ox by its horn and the man by his word.

*Palabras
medidas son
bien recibidas.*

The right words
are always
welcome.

Speech
Habla

El poco hablar es oro, el mucho hablar es lodo.

Few words are gold, more of them are mud.

No hay cosas más baratas que las buenas palabras.
Fine words come cheap.

Palabras y plumas se las lleva el viento.
Words and feathers are carried away by the wind.

Sanan llagas y no malas palabras.
Wounds heal, wounding words don't.

Palabra dada, casi sagrada.
Words spoken must not be broken.

Antes de hablar, es bueno pensar.
Think before you speak.

Piensa antes de hablar y no hablar antes de pensar.
Think before talking, don't talk before thinking.

Habla poco para no decir disparates.
He says little so that what he says will not be foolish.

Hablar poco y mal, ya es mucho.
Say a little poorly and it's a lot.

Que hable para ahora o calle para siempre.
Speak now or forever hold your peace.

El que habla mucho, pronto calla.
Who talks too much will soon be silenced.

Speech
Habla

Haga quien hiciere, calle quien lo viere y malhaya
quien lo dijere.
Do what you please, don't head others' pleas—
to hell with anyone who disagrees.

Donde hablan letras, callan barbas.
When learned words speak, rude words listen.

Dos habladores nunca viajarán juntas.
Two talkers will not go far together.

Más moscas se cogen con miel que con hiel.
More flies stick to honey than to gall.
(Sweet talk is more effective than bitterness.)

El hablar es más facil que el probar.
It's easier to say something than to prove it.

Hablen cartas y callen barbas.
Save your talk for letters and you'll keep traps closed.

Hay quien mucho cacarea y nunca pone un huevo.
A lot of people cackle but never lay an egg.

No toda gallina que cacarea pone huevo.
Not every hen that cackles lays an egg.

De la abundancia del corazón, habla la boca.
A full heart overflows in speech.

El mucho hablar
descompone.

Too much talk
can spoil
anything.

Speech
Habla

*De haber
hablado se
arrepintieron
muchos; de
ser callado,
ninguno.*

Many regret
having spoken;
none regrets
keeping
still.

Cuando hables, cuida con quien, de qué, cómo,
cuándo y dónde.
*When you speak, be careful with whom, about what,
and how, when, and where.*

Lo que en el corazón está, de la boca sale.
What is in your heart will come out of your mouth.

La lengua guarda el pescuezo.
You can use your tongue to save your neck.

No tener pelos en la lengua.
Not having hair on the tongue.

No me importa si son peras o duraznos.
I don't care if they are pears or peaches.
(I don't care what you say.)

Mucho ruido, pocas nueces.
A lot of noise for so few nuts.

Salir con domingo siete.
Come out with Sunday the seventh.
(To utter an impertinent statement.)

Quien dice lo que no debe, oye lo que no quiere.
*Say what shouldn't be said and you'll hear what
shouldn't be heard.*

Silence
Silencio

En boca cerrada no entran moscas.
Flies can't enter a closed mouth.

Con el hombre callado, mucho cuidado.
Never trust a man who doesn't talk.

El que calla, otorga.
Who says nothing says "yes."

Si de alguién te quieres vengar, has de callar.
Silence is the best revenge.

Dar la callada por respuesta.
Answer with silence.

Guárdate de hombre que no habla y de perro que
no ladra.
*Beware the man who doesn't speak and the dog that
doesn't bark.*

Guárdate del agua mansa.
Be careful around still waters.

Vale más callar que locamente hablar.
It's better to say nothing than to say something stupid.

*Bueno es hablar
pero mejor es
callar.*

Speech is good,
but silence is
better.

Custom & Law
Costumbre y leyes

Buena memoria es
la escritura, pues
para siempre
dura.

Writing has a good
memory, it lasts
forever.

La costumbre hace ley.
Custom becomes law.

La costumbre es segunda naturaleza.
Custom is second nature.

No hay leyes sin excepción.
Every law has its exception.

Hecha la ley, hecha la trampa.
The law and the loophole were made together.

La ley del embudo: para mí lo ancho y para ti lo agudo.
*The law of the funnel: The wide part is mine, the narrow
is yours.*

Un dedo no hace mano.
One finger doesn't make a hand.
(One case doesn't make a law.)

Para las leyes, las muelles.
For laws, arms.
(The only law is the law of the gun.)

Allá van leyes donde quieren reyes.
Laws don't take the place of kings.

Donde no hay reglas, la necesidad la inventa.
When there are no laws, we have to invent them.

Los que aplican las leyes andan paso de bueyes.
Who carries out the law moves with the speed of an ox.

¡Que entre abogados te veas!
May you get caught between lawyers!
(*May you be caught in a lawsuit!*)

Cuando toma cuerpo el diablo, se disfraza de abogado.
When the devil goes to town, he dresses up like a lawyer.

Los necios y los porfiados hacen ricos a los abogados.
Fools and stubborn people make lawyers rich.

*Condiciones
rompen leyes.*

Circumstances
can break
the law.

LIFE

LA VIDA

Mientras dura, vida y dulzura.
Life and sweetness, as long as it lasts.

La vida no es puro placer.
There is more to life than leisure.
(Life is not a bed of roses.)

La juventud vive de la esperanza y la vejez de recuerdos.
Youth lives on hope and old age on memories.

No hay recuerdo que el tiempo no acabe
ni dolor que la muerte no consuma.
There is no remembrance that time will not erase
or sorrow that death will not consume.

Recordar es vivir.
To remember is to live.

Lo bailado ni quien lo quite.
Once danced, it can never be taken away.
(What's done is done.)

Music
Música

Llevar la música por dentro.
To have music within.
(*With a song in my heart.*)

El que quiere baile, que pague músico.
If you want to dance, you have to pay the piper.

Músico pagado toca mal son.
A paid-up musician plays a poor tune.
(*Don't pay until the job is done.*)

El que es buen músico, con una cuerda toca.
A good musician can play a song on just one string.

El que canta mal, bien le suena.
Your own song always sounds sweet.

Bien canta Marta, después de harta.
Martha sings well when she's full.
(*About a person who's happy after achieving a success.*)

También de dolor se canta cuando llorar no se puede.
From sorrow a song may rise when tears won't come.

En casa de músico, todos son músicos.
In a musician's house, everyone is a musician.

El que tiene el don de hablar puede cantar.
If you can talk, you can sing.

*Como me la
toquen bailo.*

I will dance to
whatever music
is played.

(I will do
whatever I
need to.)

Sunshine & Rain
Sol y lluvia

Cuando el sol sale, para todos sale.

When the sun shines, it shines for all.

(The best things in life are free.)

El sol calienta para todos.
The sun heats everyone.

¡Que tu sol sea siempre brillante!
May your sun always be bright!
(In tlanextia in tonatiuh.
      —Aztec [Nahuatl] greeting)

Donde entra el sol, no entra el doctor.
Where the sun enters, the doctor doesn't.

La tierra es del que la trabaja.
The land belongs to those who work it.
      —Emiliano Zapata, Mexican Revolutionary

Más vale poca tierra y bien arada,
que mucha y mal labrada.
Better a small plot of land, tilled and tidy,
than a whole lot of land, wild and weedy.

Con tierra, agua y tractor, cualquier pendejo es agricultor.
With land and water and tractor, any fool can be a farmer.

Sembraron vientos y cosecharán tempestades.
They have sown the wind and they shall reap the whirlwind.
      —Old Testament, Hosea, VIII, 7

Truenos sordos, agua a chorros.
Thunder roaring, rain will come pouring.

Cuando veas arañas en el suelo, habrá nubes en el cielo.
When spiders appear on the ground,
rain clouds will soon come around.
(A sign of rain among campesinos.)

*Aguacero antes de
las tres, tarde
hermosa es.*

Thunderstorm
before three, fair
the afternoon
will be.

Neblina en el cerro, seguro aguacero; neblina en el
llano, seguro verano.
Fog on the hill, the clouds will spill; fog on the plain,
sun'll be out again.

Señal cierta de que va a llover: ver la lluvia caer.
A sure sign of showers: seeing raindrops fall.

Mañana oscura, tarde segura.
Clouds at dawn, afternoon sun.

Arco iris a medio día, anuncia lluvia todo el día.
Rainbow at noon, rain won't end soon.

Día nublado, mañanita larga.
Cloudy sky, long morning.

Qué bonito es ver llover y no mojarse.
It's nice to see the rain and not get wet.
(It's okay to watch from the sidelines.)

Life
La vida

*Si vives y no te
mueres, ¿qué
más quieres?*

Vive y deja vivir.
Live and let live.

If you're alive and
not dead, what
more do you
want?

Mientras vas y vienes, vida tienes.
As long as you can move about, you're alive, without a doubt.

Nadie tiene la vida comprada.
No one has his life in his pocket.

No se alcanza la buena vida, dándose la vida buena.
You'll never have a good life by leading the good life.

Date buena vida y sentirás más la caída.
The softer your life the harder your fall.

La vida es un teatro en el que siempre triunfa el
mejor actor.
*Life is a theater in which the best actor always takes
the lead.*

Mientras vida dure, tiempo sobra.
While there's life, there's time.

No se apure y dure.
Don't hurry, you'll last longer.
(Haste makes waste.)

Birth
Nacimiento

Cuando la partera es mala, le hecha la culpa a la
luna tierna.
When the midwife is bad, she blames a pale moon.

Cuando la partera es mala, le hecha la culpa a la criatura.
When the midwife is bad, she blames the baby.

Cuando nació el ahorcado, hijito parió su madre.
*When the hanged man was born, his mother held
a baby boy.*
(People change with time.)

No le hace que nazcan chatos, nomás que respiren bien.
*It doesn't matter if babies are pug-nosed, so long as they
can breathe.*

Hijo sin dolor, madre sin amor.
Painless childbirth, loveless mother.
(People care little for what comes too easily.)

Jugando, jugando, nace un niño llorando.
Playing, playing, a baby's born crying.

*¡Nacimiento! Otro
ser por quien
llorar.*

Birth! Another
being to
cry for.

Youth
Juventud

La juventud es un mal que cura el tiempo.

Youth is an illness that time cures.

¡Juventud, divino tesoro!
—Ruben Darío, poeta Nicaragüense
Youth, divine treasure!

Leña verde, mal enciende.
Green wood makes a bad fire.

Leña verde humea y corre a la gente.
Green wood smokes and drives off folks.

El joven teme que se arrepentirá; el viejo se arrepiente de haber temido.
The young man fears he'll regret; the old man regrets that he feared.

Cuando joven de ilusiones, cuando viejo(a)
de recuerdos.
The young, filled with illusions; the old, filled with memories.

Pecados de la juventud se pagan en la vejez.
The sins of youth are paid for in old age.

Juventud ociosa, vejez trabajosa.
A youth who's lazy when old will work like crazy.

Árbol que crece torcido, jamás su rama endereza.
A tree that grows up crooked will never straighten its trunk.

Maturity
Madurez

Apenas sale del cascarón y ya quiere poner huevos.
Just hatched and already wants to lay eggs.
(*Still wet behind the ears.*)

Con el tiempo se maduran las verdes.
It takes time for green fruit to ripen.

Lo que pronto madura, poco dura.
What ripens fast doesn't last.

El que es perico, donde quiera es verde.
If you're a parrot, you'll be green wherever you go.

A la pera dura, el tiempo madura.
The pear that's not yellow with time will mellow.

Vale más una madura que cien verdes.
One ripe fruit is worth a hundred green ones.

El que quiere llegar a viejo, debe comenzar temprano.

If you want to reach old age, better start out early.

Age
Vejez

Son más calientes las tardes que las mañanas.

Afternoons are warmer than mornings.

(Life begins at noon; life begins at forty.)

Si quieres vivir sano, hazte viejo temprano.
To clean up your act, be old before the fact.
(*Wisdom comes with age.*)

Come poco, bebe el doble, duerme el triple, ríe cuatro veces y llegarás a viejo.
Eat little, drink twice as much, sleep three times as much, laugh four times as much, and you'll live to a ripe old age.

Almuerza mucho, come más, cena poco y vivirás.
Eat a hearty breakfast, more at lunch, and less at dinner, and you'll live to a ripe old age.

Acuéstate a las seis, levántate a las seis;
y vivirás diez veces diez.
Retire at six, arise at six again:
You will live to be ten times ten.

Ninguno tiene más edad que la que representa.
You're only as old as you look.

Buena vida, arrugas trae.
A good life brings out wrinkles.

Buena vida, arrugas estira.
A good life smoothes out wrinkles.

Cana engaña, diente miente, arruga desengaña.
Gray hair can be deceiving and teeth can be false,
but wrinkles never lie.

Las canas salen de ganas pero las arrugas sacan de duda.
Gray hair can fool you, but wrinkles never lie.

Canas y dientes son accidentes.
Gray hair and teeth arrive by accident.

No piensen que estoy tan viejo;
lo que tengo es mal cuidado.
I may look like an old clunker,
but I just haven't been very well maintained.

Buey viejo, surco derecho.
Old ox, straight furrow.
(Experience counts.)

El médico y el confesor, entre más viejos, mejor.
Priests and physicians: the older, the better.

Les salen canas y cuernos tanto a los viejos
como a los tiernos.
The old, not just the young and fair,
can give you horns and cause gray hair.

Las canas no quitan las ganas.
Desire doesn't fade with gray hair.
(There's snow on the roof, but fire in the furnace.)

Al viejo no se le pregunta "¿Cómo está?"
sino "¿Qué le duele?"
Don't ask an old man how he is, ask where he hurts.

El corazón no envejece, el cuero es lo que se arruga.

The heart doesn't age; it's only the skin that shrivels.

Age
Vejez

Burro viejo,
aparejo
nuevo.

Old jackass,
new harness.

(An old man
with a younger
woman.)

Viejo el mar y se mueve.
The sea is old but it's still current.

Viejo el aire y todavía sopla.
The wind is old but that doesn't stop it from blowing.

Viejos los cerros; y todavía reverdecen.
The hills are old but they still turn green.

Más viejo que Matusalén.
Older then Methuselah.

Viejo es Pedro para cabrero.
Pedro is too old to become a shepherd.
(*You can't teach an old dog new tricks.*)

Viejo que boda hace, *requiescat en pace.*
Old man with a bride at the altar—may he rest in peace.

Catarro, casamiento, cagalera y caída
son cuatro "ces" que matan al viejo.
Flu, floozies, flux, and falls are four "F"s that will flunk
an old man.
(*Lit.: A runny nose, marriage, the runs, and falls are four*
"C"s [words starting with c in Spanish] that kill the old.)

Joven es quien está sano aunque tenga ochenta años.
y es viejo el doliente, aunque sólo tenga veinte.
You're young if you're strong, even at sixty,
and old if you're sickly, even at sixteen.

Age
Vejez

La vejez, grave enfermedad es.
Old age, it's an advanced disease.

A buey viejo no le falta garrapata.
An old ox never lacks for ticks.
(Old age is a series of ills.)

Cuando el indio encanece, el español no parece.
By the time the Indian's hair's turned gray,
the Spaniard has already passed away.

El viejo que se cura, cien años dura.
Take care when old, live years untold.

Si respetas a tus mayores, te respetan tus menores.
Respect your elders, and youth will respect you.

Lo viejo guarda lo nuevo.
The old guards the new.

Honra a tus mayores y aprecia a los menores.
Honor your elders and appreciate your young.

Como te veo, me vi; como me ves, te verás.
As you are, I once was; as I am, you will be.

Aullidos de perro, anuncios de muerto.
A dog is howling, somebody's dying.

A la casa vieja no le faltan las goteras.

An old house is sure to have a few leaks.

(Old age brings aches and pains.)

Death
Muerte

Como es la vida, así es la muerte.

As there is life, so there is death.

Nadie se muere la víspera.
No one dies on the eve of his death.

Al morir no hay huir.
From dying there's no flying.

Para el último viaje no es menester equipaje.
The last voyage requires no baggage.

De la suerte y la muerte no hay quien la escape.
There's no escape from death and destiny.

Al que está desahuciado, nada le está vedado.
When hope is dead, nothing is denied.

A carrera larga, nadie se escapa.
The long race, there's no running away from it.

Todo lo bueno se acaba.
All good things must come to an end.

Al cabo de cien años, todos seremos calvos.
A hundred years from now we'll all be bald.
(*Death is the great equalizer.*)

Muerte deseada, vida durada.
Long for death, you'll have a long life.

No hay quien por otro se muera.
No one can die for another.

Death
Muerte

Cosa mala nunca muere, y si muere, no se extraña.
Bad things never die, and if they do, they're not missed.

Cosa mala nunca muere.
A bad thing never dies.

Mala hierba nunca muere.
A bad weed never dies.

No tener vela en el entierro.
Not having a candle at the burial.
(Dying poor, without friend or the last rites.)

El muerto a la sepultura y el vivo a la travesura.
The dead to the tomb, the living to tomfoolery.

El muerto al pozo y el vivo al gozo.
The dead to interment and the living to enjoyment.

El muerto al pozo y el vivo al negocio.
The dead to the pine box and the living to the cash box.

El muerto al hoyo y el vivo al bollo.
While the dead go to the grave, the living misbehave.

El muerto y el arrimado al tercer día apestan.
Dead bodies and deadbeats stink after three days.

Donde lloran está el muerto.
Look for tears and you will find death.

*El muerto al
pozo y el vivo
al retozo.*

The dead
to the burial
ground and the
living to the
playground.

Death
Muerte

El que ha de morir a oscuras, aunque venda velas.

Even if you sell candles, you'll have to die in darkness.

El que por su gusto muere, hasta la muerte le sabe.
Who craves something to death can even taste it in the grave.

Más vale que digan aquí corrió que aquí murió.
It's better to let them say that he ran than that he died here.

Cuando el tecolote canta, el indio muere;
esto no es cierto pero sucede.
When the owl cries, an Indian dies;
not every time, but it happens.

Entre la cuna y la sepultura, no hay cosa segura.
There's no easy path from the cradle to the grave.

La muerte suele no avisar; cuando menos lo piensa, ahí está.
Death never knocks, it just walks in when least expected.

¿Dónde está, oh muerte, tu victoria? ¿Dónde está, oh muerte, tu aguijón?
O death, where is thy sting? O grave, where is thy victory?
   —New Testament, I Corinthians, xv, 55

Como se vive se muere.
As you live so shall you die.

Murió como los marranos, a gusto de todos.
He died like a swine, making everybody happy.

El pescado muere por la boca.
A fish dies through its mouth.

Death
Muerte

A mí no me espanta el muerto, aunque salga a media noche.
Death can't frighten me, even if it comes at midnight.

Achaques quiere la muerte para llevarse al difunto.
Death wants diseases to carry off the dead.
(Death needs no excuses to take the corpse.)

Muerta como mi abuela.
Dead as my grandmother.
(Dead as a doornail.)

El que no se muere, se vuelve a ver.
If I don't die, I'll be back again.

Eres bueno para la muerte.
You are good for death.
(A rebuke to someone who is late performing an errand.)

Hay remedio contra todo, menos la muerte.
There is a cure for everything except death.

Unos van al duelo y otros al buñuelo.
Some die by duels, others by doughnuts.

Es mejor ser vivo y barbón que muerto y rasurado.
It is better to be alive bearded than dead clean-shaven.

El que te da un hueso no quiere verte morir.
Whoever throws you a bone doesn't want to see you die.

Muerto está el ausente y vivo el presente.

Death is absence, alive is presence.

(The past is gone, live for the present.)

Death
Muerte

El panteón está lleno de limpios, tragones y valientes.

The graveyard is full of blameless, brave, and greedy people.

De que se muera mi padre y morirme yo, que muera mi padre que es más viejo.
Between my father or me dying, better my father who is older.

De que se muera mi abuela y morirme yo, que se muera mi abuela que es más vieja.
Between my grandmother or me dying, better my grandmother who is older.

Haciendo por la vida que la muerte llega sola.
When death comes calling, it arrives alone.

Hay muertos que no hacen ruidos y son mayores sus penas.
There are dead who make no noise, and their complaints are the loudest.

Los muertos no hablan.
Dead men tell no tales.

Las hojas en el árbol no duran toda la vida.
The leaves on a tree don't last forever.

Llegando al campo santo no hay calaveras plateadas.
When you get to the cemetery, you won't find any gold-plated skulls.

Death
Muerte

Al vivo todo le falta; al muerto, todo le sobra.
The living need everything; the dead, nothing.

Seis pies de tierra hacen iguales a todos las personas.
Six feet of earth make all people equal.

Muerto de sed al borde del agua.
Dead from thirst alongside the water.
(Water, water everywhere but ne'er a drop to drink.
　　—S. T. Coleridge, *The Ancient Mariner*)

*No hay nada fuerte
para la muerte.*

Nothing is as
strong as
death.

Water
Agua

*¡Lo del agua
al agua!*

Lo que en el agua viene, en el agua se va.
What comes with the water, leaves with the water.

Easy come,
easy go.

Cuando el río suena agua lleva.
When the river babbles it is bearing water.

(Let it go.)

Nadie diga: "de esta agua no beberé."
Let no one say, "From this water I will not drink."

Ahogarse en un baso de agua.
To drown in a glass of water.

Hacer una tormenta de un vaso de agua.
To make a storm out of a glass of water.

No se puede unir agua con aceite.
Oil and water don't mix.

Algo tendrá el agua cuando la bendicen.
The water must have something when they bless it.
(There's something fishy here.)

Agua que no has de beber, déjala correr.
Water you aren't going to drink, let it run.

Agua que no has de usar, déjala pasar—ahora se
puede vender.
Water you don't use, let it run—now you can sell it.

Water
Agua

El río se desborda y mata; el arroyo riega y canta.
The river overflows and kills; the stream waters and sings.

Del agua mansa me libre Dios, que de la recia me libro yo.
From gentle waters, God save me;
from the rapids, I'll save myself.
(Still waters run deep—beware of the meek when aroused.)

Debajo del agua mansa está la mejor corriente.
Beneath the gentle water is the stronger current.

En río quedo, no metas ni un dedo.
In still waters don't even stick a finger.

Como burro de aguadro, cargado de agua y
muerto de sed.
Like the burro of a water seller, loaded with water
and dying of thirst.

Nunca digas de esta agua no beberé.
Never say I will not drink from this water.
(Never say never.)

De gota a gota, la mar se agota.
Drop by drop the ocean drops.

*El agua es blanda
y la piedra dura,
pero gota a
gota hace
cavadura.*

The water is soft
and the rock is
hard, but drop
by drop the
water will
create a
cavity.

LIFE'S PLEASURES

LAS ALEGRÍAS

Goza de tu poco mientras busca más el loco.
Be happy with your little bit:
Only a fool strives for all he can get.

Más vale poco y bueno, que mucho y malo.
Better little and good, than a lot and bad.

Más vale que sobre que no que falte.
Better too much than not enough.

El que nada desperdicia nunca carece.
One who doesn't waste will never lack.
(Waste not, want not.)

Lo poco agrada, lo mucho enfada.
A little pleases, a lot displeases.

Cada uno extiende la pierna hasta donde llega la sábana.
We stretch our legs only as far as the sheet reaches.
(*Do not live beyond your means.*)

Por un gustazo, un trancazo.
For every pleasure there is a punishment.

Chiquito pero sabroso.
Only a little, but delicious.

Dinamita viene en pequeños paquetes.
Dynamite comes in small packages.

La esencia fina se vende en frasco pequeño.
Fine perfume is sold in small bottles.
(*Good things come in small packages.*)

Muchos pocos hacen un mucho.
A lot of a little makes a lot.

Poquito porque es bendito.
Only a little because it is blessed.
(*An excuse to give someone little food, alcohol, or medicine.*)

El que se hace miel, se lo comen las abejas.
Who turns into honey will be eaten by bees.

*Más vale poco de lo
mejor que mucho
de lo peor.*

Better a little of
the best than a lot
of the worst.

Sweetness & Joy
Dulzura y alegría

El placer engorda más que el comer.

Pleasure is more fattening than food.

Si no tienes dinero en la bolsa, ten miel en la boca.
If you have no money in your pocket, have honey in your mouth.

A veces lo dulce amarga si con disgusto se traga.
Even something sweet can be bitter if taken when angry.

Haz la noche noche y el día día y vivirás con alegría.
Make the night night and the day day and you will live with happiness.

Alegría secreta, candela muerta.
Happiness that is secret: a candle that is extinguished.

Las flores contentan pero no alimentan.
Flowers make you happy but you can't live on them.

Noche alegre, mañanita triste.
Night of joy, morning of regret.

Si no puedes lo que quieras, quiere lo que puedas.
If you can't have what you want, want what you have.

Tastes
Gustos

De gustos, no hay nada escrito.
On tastes, nothing is written.
(*There's no disputing taste.*)

Gusto con gusto, siempre es gusto.
Pleasure you can taste is always a pleasure.

¿Qué sería de las feas o feos si no hubiera malos gustos?
What would become of the ugly if it weren't for bad taste?

A tu gusto, mula, y le daban de palos.
As you like, mule—and they beat her.
(*You asked for it.*)

Entre las gentes hay mil gustos diferentes.
People have a thousand different preferences.

Hay que gustos de gustos.
There is delight in delight.

Hay gustos que merecen palos.
Some tastes deserve a beating.

Nunca llueve a gusto de todos.

It never rains to everybody's satisfaction.

(You can't please everyone.)

Appetite
Hambre

El hambre es lo bueno, no la comida.
Hunger is what is good, not the meal.

No hay mejor salsa que el hambre.
Hunger is the best sauce.

Para el buen hambre, no hay mal pan.
For a good hunger, there is no bad bread.

El que hambre tiene, en pan piensa.
One who is hungry thinks of bread.

El que tiene hambre, en tortillas piensa.
One who is hungry thinks of tortillas.

De la flor viene el olor y de la fruta el sabor.
*From the flower comes the fragrance, from the fruit
comes the taste.*

Carro nuevo y con la tripa clara.
A new car and an empty stomach.

Cuando no hay carne de lomo, de toda como.
When there's no sirloin to eat, I will take any meat.

Primero es comer, que cristiano ser.
A Christian life to meet, the first thing is to eat.

Panza llena, corazón contento.
Full belly, happy heart.

Migajas también son pan y buen alimento dan.
Crumbs are bread too, and will also nourish you.

Come pan, bebe agua y vivirás larga vida.
Eat bread, drink water, and you will live a long life.

Come y le da a uno sueño, despierta y le da a uno hambre.
Eat and you get sleepy, wake up and you get hungry.

Nunca ha de faltar un pelo en la comida.
There's always a hair in the food.

Gallina vieja hace buen caldo.
An old hen makes a good soup.

Arroz que no se menea, se quema.
Unstirred rice will burn.

Vale más que sobre y no que falte.
It is better to have leftovers than not to have enough.

Más vale pan duro que ninguno.
Better stale bread than none.

Pan con pan, comida de tontos.
Bread with bread: a fool's meal.

Contigo, pan y cebolla.
With you, bread and onions.
(I'll stick by you through thick and thin.)

*Donde comen dos,
comerán tres.*

Where two eat,
three can eat.

(There's always
room for one
more.)

No puedes sopear con gordas ni hacer tacos con tostadas.
*You can't dunk fresh tortillas nor make tacos with dry
tostadas.*
(*You can't have it both ways.*)

El comal le dijo a la olla — "¡Que cola tan más prieta
tienes!"
The griddle said to the pot, "What a black tail you have!"

El comal le dijo a la olla — "¡Que tiznada estás!"
The griddle said to the pot, "You are very black!"

No te hagas boca chiquita.
Don't pretend to be a small mouth.
(*Don't be shy at the table.*)

La gallina que come en tu casa y pone en la ajena,
no es buena.
*A hen that eats in your house and lays in another's
is no good.*

Llamar al pan, pan y al vino, vino.
Call bread bread, and wine wine.
(*Call it as you see it.*)

El camino a la boca nadie se equivoca.
No one errs on the road to their mouth.

A pan duro, diente agudo.
Hard bread, sharp tooth.

Antes de que se lo coman los gusanos, que se lo
coman los cristianos.
Before the worms get to it, let Christian folk eat.

Cuando hay para carne es vigilia.
When there is money for meat, it is Lent.

Bien barato sería el pan, sin comer el holgazán.
Bread would be dirt cheap if freeloaders didn't eat.

No hay caldo que no se enfríe.
There is no soup that doesn't get cold.

En mesa ajena, la tripa llena.
On another's bill, eat your fill.

A comer y a misa, a la primera llamada.
To the table and to mass, you must come when first asked.

No sólo de pan vive el hombre.
Man does not live by bread alone.

En casa sin harina, todo se vuelve una muina.
In a home without flour, everyone's dour.

El rico come cuando quiere y el pobre cuando puede.
The rich eat when they want, the poor when they can.

Bueno el culantro, pero no tanto.
Coriander is good—but not too much.

*De que te haga
malo o que se
heche a perder,
mejor que te
haga malo.*

If something can
make you ill or
spoils you, it's
better that
it make
you ill.

*No hay mejor
bocado que'l
robado.*

There is no better
snack than a
stolen one.

En tu casa no tienes sardinas y en la ajena pides gallina.
*At home you don't have sardines, at your neighbor's you
ask for chicken.*

De la mano a la boca, se pierde la sopa.
From the hand to the mouth, your soup can go south.

Se hizo miel y se la comieron las moscas.
She made herself honey and was eaten by flies.

No sabe bien la cena que se come en casa ajena.
A meal in another's house doesn't taste as good.

El mismo cuchillo que corta el pan, corta dedos.
The same knife that cuts bread cuts fingers.

Al escuchar disparates: "¿y con esa misma boca comes?"
*Upon hearing obscenities: "Do you eat with that same
mouth?"*

Depués de un buen taco, un buen tabaco.
After a good taco, a good tobacco.

Sólo mis chicharrones truenan.
Only my cracklings make noise.
(I'm the boss here.)

Sólo la cuchara sabe lo que hay dentro de la olla.
Only the spoon knows what's inside the pot.
(Everyone knows his own thoughts.)

Quien mucho come, mucho bebe; quien mucho bebe,
mucho duerme; y quien mucho duerme, poco lee,
poco sabe y poco vale.
Who eats too much, drinks too much; who drinks too
much sleeps too much; and who sleeps too much reads
little, knows little, and is worth little.

A la boca amarga, la miel le sabe a retama.
To a bitter mouth, honey tastes sour.

De las tunas, come una o dos; que si muchas,
¡Válgame Dios!
Of prickly pears, eat one or two; if you eat many:
"God help me!"
(*Prickly pears can be laxative.*)

Más mató la cena que sanó Avicena.
The dinner killed more people than Avicena cured.
(*Avicena, 980–1037, was an Arab physician and*
philosopher.)

Entre col y col, lechuga.
Between cabbage and cabbage, lettuce.

La carne pegada al hueso es la más sabrosa.
Meat close to the bone is the most delicious.

El más chimuelo masca rieles.
The one with the fewest teeth eats rails.
(*The thinnest eats most; don't underestimate anyone.*)

Ya comí, ya bebí,
ya no me siento
bien aquí.

I drank, I ate,
and now I
don't feel
so great.

Food & Cooking
Cocina

A la mejor cocinera se le ahuma la olla.

Even the best cook can ruin the pot.

Comer para vivir y no vivir para comer.
Eat to live, don't live to eat.

Chilaquiles aquí, enchiladas allá.
Chilaquiles here, enchiladas there.
(*It's the same old story.*)

Comen frijoles y eructan pollo.
They eat beans and burp chicken.

Olla que hierve mucho se quema o se derrama.
A pot that boils too much will burn or boil over.

El que no desperdicia nunca carece.
Who never wastes never lacks.

En todas partes se cuecen habas.
Beans are cooked everywhere.
(*It's the same the world over.*)

A falta de pan, tortillas.
When there's no bread: tortillas.

No hay que poner todos los huevos en una canasta.
Don't put all your eggs in one basket.
　　—Benjamin Franklin, *Poor Richard's Almanac*

No me suene el maíz que no soy gallina.
Don't crack corn in front of me, I'm not a chicken.
(*Don't tell me, I'm not interested.*)

Olla que mucho hierve, sabor pierde.
A pot that boils over loses its flavor.

El que come y canta, loco se levanta.
Who eats and sings a tune wakes up crazy as a loon.

El que tiene que comer, se olvida del que no tiene.
The person who has food to eat forgets the one who doesn't have anything.

No le tengan miedo al chile aunque lo vean colorado.
Don't be afraid of chile just because it looks red.

Chile agitado peligro de regar las semillas.
Shake the chile and you risk losing the seeds.

Picoso pero sabroso.
Hot but delicious.

Pleitos con todos menos la cocinera.
Fight anyone except the cook.

Harto ayuna el que mal come.
He who eats badly fasts well.

Sal con tomates, jamón de pobres.
Tomatoes with salt are ham to the poor.

Si quieres ser bien servido, sírvete tú mismo.
If you want good service, serve yourself.

*Con la tripa llena,
ni bien huyes ni
bien peleas.*

You can't flee and
you can't fight
with a full
stomach.

Food & Cooking
Cocina

*Da Dios
almendras al
que no tiene
muelas.*

God gives
almonds to those
who no longer
have molars.

(When prosperity
comes too late
in life.)

Me he de comer esa tuna aunque me espine la mano.
I'll eat that prickly pear even if it pricks my hand.

No se puede chiflar y comer pinole al mismo tiempo.
You can't whistle and eat pinole at the same time.
(Pinole *is a powdery sweet corn that one can choke on.*)
(*You can't do two things at the same time.*)

El que tiene más saliva come más pinole.
The one who has the most saliva eats the most pinole.

Juntos pero no revueltos.
Together but not mixed.

Hazte sordo y ponte gordo.
Feign deafness and grow fat.
(*Face lies with indifference.*)

Al rey se le pone la mesa: si quiere come y si no, lo deja.
*The table is set for the king: If he wants to eat, he will;
if not, he will leave it alone.*
(*Let a person accept or reject.*)

El comer y el rascar, todo consiste en empezar.
In eating and scratching, beginning's the main thing.

Da atole con el dedo.
Gives gruel with a finger.
(*People who give words of praise instead of delivering
promises.*)

Cuesta más el caldo que las albóndigas.
The soup costs more than the meatballs.

Usted no será de harina, pero me huele a bizcocho.
*You may not be made out of flour, but you smell like
a biscuit.*

Comida hecha, visita deshecha.
Comida acabada, compañía deshechada.
Meal done, company gone.

A todo le llaman cena aunque sea un taco con sal.
Anything can be called dinner, even a taco with salt.

Al nopal lo van a ver sólo cuando tiene tunas.
They only visit the cactus when it has prickly pears.

Ahí verás si mueres de hambre o comes lo que te den.
*Let's see whether you die of hunger or if you'll eat what
you have been served.*

En el modo de cortar el pan se conoce al tragón.
The manner of cutting bread is a sign of a glutton.

Entre dos cocineras sale aguado el mole.
With two cooks, the mole comes out too thin.
(*Too many cooks spoil the soup.*)

Valen más frijoles con hambre que chinitos con manteca.
Beans with hunger are better than refried beans with lard.

Food & Cooking
Cocina

Ni amor al caldo, ni piedad a los frijoles.

Neither love the soup nor pity the beans.

(Both are good.)

De que se pierda o que te haga daño, mejor que te haga daño.
Between throwing it away or making you ill, better that it make you ill.

Tú le das sabor al caldo.
You give the soup good taste.

En la puerta del horno se quema el pan.
The bread is burnt at the oven door.

Eres lo que comes.
You are what you eat.

Las cuentas claras y el chocolate espeso.
The accounts clear and the chocolate thick.
(*Call a spade a spade.*)

Chocolate
Chocolate

Estar como agua para chocolate.
To be like water for chocolate.
(*To be so passionate that you're boiling over,*
like water ready for chocolate.)

Contigo la milpa es rancho y el atole, champurrado.
With you the corn field is a ranch and gruel is a
chocolate drink.

A cualquier cosa le llaman chocolate los patrones.
Employers will call anything a chocolate.

A todo le sienta el tomate, menos a las gachas
y al chocolate.
Anything goes well with tomato, except slouch hats
and chocolate.

Ni amor reanudado, ni chocolate recalentado.
Neither renewed love, nor reheated chocolate.

Una sopa de tu propio chocolate.
A soup from your very own chocolate.

Más vale atole con sonrisas que chocolate con lágrimas.
Better to have gruel with a smile than chocolate with tears.

Ni chocolate
recalentado,
ni amor
parchado.

Neither
warmed-over
chocolate nor a
patched-up
romance.

(Some things will
never be the
same again.)

Alcohol & Drink
Alcohol y beber

En este mundo mesquino, cuando hay para pan no hay para vino.

In this miserable world, when there is enough for bread, there isn't enough for wine.

Quien de la cantina va y viene, dos casas mantiene.
Who goes back and forth from the bar, keeps two homes.

Los tres estados de la embriaguez son: león, mono y cerdo.
The three stages of inebriation are: lion, ape, and pig.

Para todo mal, mezcal, y para todo bien también.
For all ailments, mezcal, and for all good also.

Cena de vino, desayuno de agua.
Wine at dinner, water at breakfast.

Si el vino te tiene loco, déjalo poquito a poco.
If wine is giving you fits, let it go, bit by bit.

Dulce licor, bello tormento,
¿Que haces afuera? ¡Vamos pa' dentro!
Sweet liquor, beautiful torment,
what are you doing outside? Come inside!

No hay borracho que coma lumbre.
No drunk will eat fire.
(Some things no one will do.)

El vino de buena cuba no necesita bandera.
Wine from a good cask needs no label.

El vino que es bueno no ha de menester pregonero.
Good wine does not need advertising.

Hay que acabar con el vino antes de que el vino acabe conmigo.
I have to finish the wine before the wine finishes me.

El vino hace insolente al hombre; las bebidas fuertes lo alborotan.
Wine makes a man insolent, strong drink makes him rage.
   —Old Testament, Proverbs, xx, 1

El vino embota el entendimiento.
Wine dulls all understanding.

Comamos y bebamos que mañana moriremos.
Let us eat and drink, for tomorrow we shall die.
   —Old Testament, Isaiah, xxii, 13

A quien no le gusta el vino, sólo se hace su castigo.
A person who doesn't like wine is only punishing himself.

El agua es para los bueyes, el vino para los hombres.
Water is for oxen, wine is for men.

Hay que morir borracho para no sentirse tan gacho.
Be drunk when you die so the pain will go by.

Alcohol &
Drink
*Alcohol y
beber*

*No bebas sin ver ni
firmes sin leer.*

Don't drink
without seeing
nor sign without
reading.

Alcohol & Drink
Alcohol y beber

Debajo de mala capa suele haber un buen bebedor.

Beneath a shabby cape is usually a good drinker.

Boca de borracho, oídos de cantinero.
Mouth of a drunk, ears of bartender.

De borrachos y panzones está lleno el panteón.
Drunks and fat bellies fill the cemetery.

Contra las muchas penas, las copas llenas; contra las pocas penas, llenas las copas.
Against the many sorrows, goblets full; against a few sorrows, full goblets.

Del borracho que pretende de valiente, se ríe la gente.
A drunk who pretends courage makes people laugh.

No es borracho el que ha bebido, sino el que sigue bebiendo.
The one who drinks is not the drunk—it's the one who keeps on drinking.

Donde entra beber, sale saber.
Where drinking enters, wisdom leaves.

Después de beber, cada quien dice su parecer.
After drinking, everyone speaks his mind.

Barril sin fondo.
A barrel without a bottom.

Alcohol & Drink
Alcohol y beber

Emborracha al hombre si lo quieres conocer.
Get a man drunk if you really want to know him.

Levantar el codo.
To hoist the elbow.
(Description of a drinker.)

La persona embriagada, sin irse se ha ausentado.
Without leaving, the inebriated person takes leave.

Más vale emborracharse que lidiar con un borracho.
It is better to get drunk than to have to deal with a drunk.

Sin beber y comer no hay placer.

Without food and drink there is no pleasure.

Sleep
Dormir

El sueño es
alimento de
los pobres.

Dreams are
nourishment for
the poor.

Antes que resuelvas nada, consúltalo con la almohada.
Before making any important decision, consult your pillow.

A buen sueño no hay mal cama.
For sleepiness, there is no bad bed.

No hay mejor colchón que un buen sueño.
There is no better mattress than a good sleep.

Un petate es buen colchón para aquel que lo tumba
el sueño.
A mat makes a good mattress when you're falling asleep.

La mala cama hace la noche larga.
An uncomfortable bed makes for a long night.

En cama extraña, mal se juntan las pestañas.
In a strange bed, eyelashes don't easily come together.
(It's hard to sleep in a strange bed.)

Gato que duerme no caza ratón.
A sleeping cat catches no mice.

¡Bendito sea el que inventó dormir!
Blessed be he who invented sleep!

Planchar oreja.
Ironing an ear.

Health
Salud

Salud y alegría crían belleza.
Health and happiness create beauty.

No te apures pa' que dures.
For long life, avoid strife.

Coja es la pena, más llega.
Pain limps, but it arrives.

Todo se pega, menos la salud.
Everything is contagious except good health.

Curarse en salud.
Get well in health.

Aplaca tus deseos y alargarás tu vida.
Satisfy your desires and you will lengthen your life.

El cuerpo acepta lo que la mente no comprende.
The body accepts what the mind does not understand.

Eres lo que no excretas.
You are what you don't excrete.

El estreñido muere de cursio.
The constipated person will die of diarrhea.

En comiendo mucho y meando claro, manda a la porra al cirujano.
Pissing clear and eating well, tell the doctor to go to hell.

Salud, dinero y amor, y tiempo para gozarlas.

Health, money and love, and time to enjoy them.

Health
Salud

*Con lo que sana
Susana, cae
enferma
Juana.*

What cures
Susana, makes
Juana ill.

(One person's
potion is
another person's
poison.)

Al enfermo que es de vida, hasta el agua le es medicina.
For the invalid destined to endure, even water can be a cure.

Más vale salud que dinero.
Better to have health than money.

Cuando Dios quiere, hasta el agua es medicina.
When God wishes, even water is medicine.

Jesús te favorezca y el diablo te aborrezca.
May Jesus favor you and the devil hate you.
(*Expression when the person next to you sneezes.*)

¡Jesús, María y José!
Jesus, Mary, and Joseph!
(*Expression when the person next to you sneezes.*)

La que come manzana, se cría sana.
A person who eats apples will grow up healthy.

Lo que es bueno para el hígado no es bueno para el bazo.
What is good for the liver is not good for the spleen.
(*What is poison for one is medicine for another.*)

Más vale sano que pagarle al cirujano.
Better enjoy good health than give the surgeon your wealth.

Opinan muchos que los baños traen menos bienes
que daños.
Many think bathing more ruinous than beneficial.

THE SEXES

LOS SEXOS

El consejo de la mujer es poco y el que no lo escucha es loco.
Though the woman speaks but a little bit,
if the man doesn't listen, he hasn't much wit.

Para el amor no hay fronteras.
Love knows no borders.

¿En qué bodegón hemos comido juntos?
In what cheap dive have we eaten together?
(Haven't we met before?)

Men &
Women
Hombres y
mujeres

*La mujer es fuego;
el hombre, estopa;
viene el Diablo
y sopla.*

The woman's a
fire, the man is
quick tinder;
in comes the
devil and
blows on an
ember.

El hombre debe ser feo, fuerte y formal.
A man should be homely, hardy, and honorable.

Al hombre bueno no le busques abolengo.
Don't search for a good man's ancestry.

Al hombre ni todo el amor ni todo el dinero.
No man can have all the love nor all the money.

Dados, mujeres y vino, sacan al hombre del buen camino.
Wine, women, and gambling set many men to rambling.

El que a los veinte no es valiente, a los treinta no es
casado, y a los cuarenta no es rico, es gallo que clavó
el pico.
*A man who's not daring at twenty, married at thirty, and
rich at forty is a rooster with his beak stuck shut.*

Caballo que llene las piernas, gallo que llene las manos
y mujer que llene los brazos.
*A horse that fits between your legs, a rooster that fits in
your hands, and a woman that fits in your arms.*

Pistola, caballo y mujer, tener bien o no tener.
*Guns, horses, and women: Don't take them if you can't
take care of them.*

Más vale muchacho roto que viejo con pantalones.
Better a youth in rags than an old man in fancy pants.

A las mujeres y a los charcos no hay que andarles
con rodeos.
*Women and puddles: Don't go out of your way to get
around them.*

*No hay bonita sin
pero, ni fea sin
gracia.*

La cobija y la mujer, suavecitas han de ser.
A blanket and a woman should be nice and soft.

There is no
beautiful woman
without a flaw,
nor an ugly one
without some
favor.

Es más facil contener la corriente de un río, que a la
mujer cuando se obstina.
It's easier to oppose a river than the will of a woman.

Mujer que no tiene tacha, chapalea el agua y no se moja.
*A woman who's innocent can splash around in the water
and not get wet.*

Es tan fácil enamorarse de una mujer rica como de
una pobre.
*It's as easy to fall in love with a rich woman as it is
with a poor one.*

La mujer y la sardina, entre más chica, mas fina.
Women and sardines: the smaller, the finer.

El animal más raro y bruto es el hombre.
The rarest and stupidest animal is man.

*El chiste no es
ser hermosa
sino saber
presumir.*

The trick is not to
be beautiful, but
to know how to
fake it.

Feo pero con suerte.
Ugly but lucky.

La suerte de la fea, la bonita la desea.
The luck of the plain, the fair wants to gain.

El hombre como el oso, entre más feo, más hermoso.
Man is like a bear—the uglier, the handsomer.

Toda mujer tiene sus cinco minutos
All women have their five minutes of glory.

Ni fea que espante, ni hermosa que encante.
Not so ugly she's blinding, nor so fair she's spellbinding.

La hermosura poco dura.
Looks don't last.
(Beauty is only skin deep.)

La virtud es hermosa en las más feas y el vicio es feo
en las más hermosas.
*Virtue flatters the ugliest woman as vice flaws the
most beautiful.*

Hermosura sin bondad, más que un bien, es un mal.
*Good looks without goodness: more of a curse than
a blessing.*

Hermosura y castidad, muy raras veces van juntas.
Beauty and chastity rarely go together.

Una mujer hermosa puede tener vanidad, pero una
fea tiene presunción.
*A beautiful woman can be proud, but an ugly one can
be presumptuous.*

El hambre las tumba y vanidad las levanta.
Hunger knocks them down but vanity picks them up.
(Said of thin, pretentious women.)

Compuesta, no hay mujer fea.
Made up, there is no ugly woman.

Más tira moza que soga.
A pretty girl has more pull than a rope.

Estiran más tetas que carretas.
Bustlines move more men than bus lines.

Jala más un par de nalgas que una yunta de bueyes.
A nice ass can haul more than a pair of oxen.

Un cabello de mujer tira más que cien yuntas be bueyes.
*A single strand of a woman's hair is stronger than a
hundred pair of oxen.*

*La mujer tiene
al hombre a la
distancia que
ella quiere.*

A woman can hold
a man at whatever
distance she
wants.

Looks &
Longing
Hermosura y lujuria

Como hay unos, hay otros.

Where there's one, there are sure to be others.

(There is always someone better.)

Más vale caer en gracia que caer gracioso.
It's better to fall into favor than into folly.
(*It's better to please than to play the fool.*)

¿Por qué estás pisando en la tierra, si tu lugar es el cielo?
Why are you walking on earth, you belong in heaven?
(*Example of a "piropo," a compliment to a woman.*)

¡Ay que bonita piedra para darme un tropezón!
Ah! What a precious stone to trip over!
(*Example of a "piropo," a compliment to a woman.*)

Fondo salido busca marido.
It shows—you're looking for a man.
(*Said to a woman whose slip is sticking out.*)

Gallo, caballo y mujer, por su raza has de conocer.
A rooster, a horse, and a woman should be chosen for their type.

Date a deseo y olerás a polvillo.
Give in to lust and you'll smell like dust.

Hasta el pelo más delgado hace su sombra en el suelo.
Even the thinnest hair casts a shadow on the ground.

Pajar viejo arde más presto.
Old haystacks are quick to burst into flame.

*Manos frías,
corazón ardiente.*

Cold hands,
warm heart.

Pajar viejo encendio, malo es apagar.
Let in an old flame, you'll have a hard time putting it out.

Las lumbres que yo he prendido no las apaga cualquiera.
The fires I have started, not just anyone can extinguish.

Bajo las cenizas, rescoldos quedan.
Beneath the ashes, a spark remains.

Bajo este cenizo pelo, arde un rescoldo.
Beneath this ashen hair, an ember's still alight.

Hacer de tripas corazón.
To make a heart out of guts.
(To create love from courage.)

Me parte el corazón.
It breaks my heart.

Me parte el alma.
It breaks my soul.

Donde hubo fuego, cenizas quedan.
Ashes remain where there once was fire.

¿Si no te animas para qué te arrimas?
If you aren't willing, why do you come near?

Love
Amor

*De amor y amor,
sólo amor.*

From love plus
love, only
love.

Amor primero, amor postrero.
Love, first and last.

Compañía de dos, compañía de Dios.
Company of two, company of God.
(Where two are together, God is there.)

Amor y viento, se va uno y viene un ciento.
Love, like a breeze—when one is gone a hundred appear.

El que te quiere te hace llorar.
You always hurt the one you love.

Amor, amor, nada hay peor ni mejor.
Love, love—nothing below it, nothing above.

Amor que no se atreve, no es de fuego, sino de nieve.
Love without risks is not of fire but of ice.

Amor que no es atrevido, lo que logra es el olvido.
A love that isn't bold soon grows old.

De enamorado a loco, hay muy poco.
In love or insane—these two things are much the same.

Amor es demencia y su médico la ausencia.
Love is dementia and its cure is absentia.

Amor no respeta ley, pero obedece a su rey o reina.
Love does not respect the law, yet it obeys its king or queen.

Love
Amor

Amor y olvido nace de descuido.
A love forgotten is born from lack of care.

Amante ausentado, amante olvidado.
Absent lover, forgotten lover.

Amor viejo y camino real, nunca se dejan de andar.
An old love and a royal road are never abandoned.

Tan lejos de ojo, tan lejos de corazón.
Out of sight, out of mind.

El sapo a la sapa la tiene por muy guapa.
The frog believes his woman frog to be beautiful.
(*Love is blind.*)

Donde hay amor, hay dolor.
Where there is love, there is pain.

Donde hay amor, no hay temor.
Where there is love, there is no fear.

Amor y aborrecimiento no quitan conocimiento.
Love and hatred have nothing to do with knowledge.

Amor que ha sido brasa, de repente vuelve a arder.
A love that has been a burning coal will soon reignite.

De los retozos resultan los mocosos.
The fun and frolic of foreplay results in snotty kids.

Donde no hay amor, no hay dolor.

Where there is no love, there is no pain.

Love
Amor

*Amor con amor
se paga.*

Love is rewarded
with love.

(Love begets
love.)

Desgraciado en el juego, afortunado en amores.
Unlucky at cards, lucky in love.

Ama bien quien nunca olvida.
He loves well who never forgets.

Ni amor al mundo, ni piedad al cielo.
Neither love the world, nor pity the heaven.
(I ask nothing from anyone.)

Se van los amores y quedan los dolores.
Love departs and the sorrows remain.

Ni sábado sin sol, ni fea sin amor.
*Neither a Saturday without sun, nor a homely
girl without love.*

Para el amor y la muerte no hay casa ni cosa fuerte.
Love and death: No house, no thing as strong.
(Love and death respect no barriers.)

El amor es un egoísmo entre dos.
Love is egoism shared by two.

En la batalla del amor, el que huye es el vencedor.
*On the battlefield of love, the one who runs away is
the winner.*

El amor y la justicia son ciegos.
Love and justice are blind.

Love
Amor

Todo es válido en el amor y en la guerra.
All is fair in love and war.

Al amor lo pintan ciego.
They paint love blind.

El amor no es como lo pintan.
Love is not the way they paint it.

Amor de lejos, amor de pendejos.
Love from afar, love for fools.

Amor viejo, ni te olvido ni te dejo.
Old love, I won't forget you nor will I leave you.

El amor para que dure debe ser disimulado.
For love to endure, it should be feigned.

No hay amor sin interés.
There is no love without self-interest.

Del amor al odio sólo hay un paso.
From love to hate is but a step.

Los yerros del amor son dignos de perdón.
The errors of love are worthy of forgiveness.

Cuando te quieren te vas, cuando te aborrecen vienes.
*When you are loved, you leave; when you are hated,
you come.*

*Querer y aborrecer
no puede a un
tiempo ser.*

Love and hate you
cannot do at the
same time.

Love
Amor

El que ama a una mujer ajena siempre anda descolorido; no por el amor que siente sino por el miedo al marido.

He who loves another man's wife is always pale: Not from the love he feels but from fear of the husband.

Amor, dinero y cuidado nunca pueden ser disimulados.
Love, money, and care can never be feigned.

Contra amor y fortuna no hay defensa alguna.
Against love and fortune there is no defense.

El dinero y el amor no permiten encubridor.
Money and love do not allow concealment.

Amor con celos causa desvelos.
Love with jealousy causes insomnia.

Con amor y aguardiente nada se siente.
With love and alcohol nothing is felt at all.

Con dos que se quieren, con uno que coma basta.
With two people in love, one eating is sufficient.

El amor es ciego.
Love is blind.

No hay amor como el primero.
There is no love like the first love.

Poco es el amor y lo vamos a gastar en celos.
So little love to waste it on jealousy.

Es poco el amor y desperdiciarlo en celos.
Love is too scarce to waste on jealousy.

Love
Amor

Amores nuevos olvidan a los viejos.
New loves make old loves forgotten.

De un viejo amor ni se olvida ni se deja.
An old love is never forgotten or dismissed.

El amor es como los pasteles, que recalentados no sirven.
Love, like pie, is no good reheated.

Dos para quererse, deben parecerse.
To like each other, be like each other.

Cada quien con su cada cual.
Everyone with his certain someone.

El carbón que es brasa, fácilmente vuelve a arder.
A charcoal that is an ember can easily burn again.

El que padece de amor, hasta con las piedras habla.
One who is lovesick will even talk to rocks.

Como ni amor le tengo, ni cuidado le pongo.
Since I don't love him, I don't care about him.

El que en un corral se cría, en un pajar se enamora.
Who is raised in a corral falls in love in a haystack.

Sólo fue llamarada de petate.
It was only a small flame from a straw bedroll.

No serás amado si de ti sólo tienes cuidado.

You will never be loved if you care only for yourself.

Love
Amor

Vale más adorada de viejo que esclava de joven.

Better adored by an old man that enslaved by a young man.

Amor, no lo parieron burros.
Love was not birthed by burros.
(*Love is not for fools.*)

Los enamorados piensan que todos tienen los ojos tapados.
Lovers think that everyone's eyes are covered.

Hoy son los amores, mañana los desengaños.
Today love, tomorrow disillusionment.

Pleitos de enamorados, presto son olvidados.
Lovers' quarrels are soon forgotten.

Single or Married?
Solterismo

Antes que te cases, mira lo que haces.
Tarry before you marry.

No des paso sin huarache.
Don't take a step without your sandals.

Al cabo no tengo mujer bonita que mantener ni
hijos llorones.
*At least I don't have a beautiful woman to support, nor
a bunch of bawling children.*

No tengo padre, ni madre, ni perro que me ladre.
I don't have a father, nor mother, nor dog to bark for me.

Quedarse como novia de rancho, vestida y alborotada.
*Stood up like a country bride, all dressed up and ready
to ride.*

Quedarse a vestir santos.
A spinster with no one to dress but the saints.

Tal para cuales, Pascuala con Pascual.
Tit for tat, every Matilda has her Matt.
(*For every man, there's a woman.*)

Cada oveja con su pareja.
Every lamb has her love.

*Habrá quien te
quiera, pero
quien te
ruegue,
nunca.*

There will always
be someone
to love you—
but don't
expect to be
begged.

Marriage
Matrimonio

El que no da de enamorado da menos de casado.

Cheap in courtship, cheaper in marriage.

Mujer de tahure (jugador), nunca te alegres, porque si hoy ganas, mañana pierdes.
If you marry a gambler, don't feel too glad; if today you win, tomorrow you lose.

Con la que entiende de atole y metate, con ésa cásate.
A woman who knows her pots and pans makes a fine catch for any man.

El que se casa, por todo pasa.
Whoever gets a ring will experience everything.

Hombre casado, siempre desconfiado.
A man with a ring is an untrustworthy thing.

El que presta la mujer para bailar o el caballo para torear, no tiene reclamo.
Who lends his wife for a dance or his horse for a bullfight cannot reclaim them.

Boda y mortaja del cielo bajan.
Weddings and shrouds come from heaven.

Quien se casa por dinero, se ha vendido entero.
When you wed for gold, you sell yourself whole.

Al que tiene mujer hermosa o castillo en la frontera, nunca le falta guerra.
He who has a beautiful wife or a castle on the border will always be at war.

Marriage
Matrimonio

Casamiento de pobres, fábrica de limosneros.
Poor people's marriage: a beggar factory.

Casamiento de pobres, fábrica de criaturas.
Poor people's marriage: a baby factory.

En casa del ruin, la mujer es alguacil.
In the home of a stingy man, the wife is in command.

Entre casados y hermanos, ninguno meta las manos.
Never get between siblings and spouses.

El casado casa quiere.
A married man wants a house.

Triste está la casa donde la gallina canta y el gallo calla.
Sad the house where the hen crows, while the rooster is silent.

Más vale bien quedada que mal casada.
Better to be happy and single than miserable and married.

Casados que no se besan, no se tienen voluntad.
Married people who don't kiss don't want each other.

Quieres saber cómo es, vive con ella un mes.
If you want to know her style, try living with her a while.

La vida de los casados los ángeles la desean.
The life of a married couple is desired by angels.

Tres cosas hechan al hombre de su casa: el humo, la gotera y la mujer vocinglera.

Three things that will drive a man from home: smoke, a leaky roof, and a loudmouthed woman.

Marriage
Matrimonio

*Lo que la loba
hace, al lobo
le place.*

The wolf's ways
his mate
sways.

El matrimonio es como la historia de los países coloniales: primero viene la conquista y luego se sueña con la independencia.
Marriage is like a colonized country: first the conquest, then the dream of independence.

Casa a tu hijo cuando quieras y a tu hija cuando puedas.
Marry off your son when you will and your daughter when you can.

El día que te cases, o te curas o te matas.
The day you wed, you either kill yourself or cure yourself.

Entre marido y mujer, nadie se debe meter.
No one should meddle in the affairs between husband and wife.

No hay boda sin tornaboda.
There is no wedding day without a day after.

En casa del mezquino, más manda la mujer que el marido.
In the home of a poor man, the wife commands more than the husband.

Lloraba la casada por su marido y ahora llora porque ha venido.
The wife cried for her husband, and now cries because he has come back.

Marriage
Matrimonio

Primera esposa, matrimonio; la segunda compañía;
la tercera, tontería.
*First wife, matrimony; the second, company; the
third, folly.*

Te casaste, te fregaste.
You got married—you got shafted.

El que enviuda y se casa, de loco se pasa.
A widower who remarries is twice a fool.

La viuda rica, con un ojo llora y con el otro repica.
*The rich widow with one eye will cry, all the while
winking the other eye.*

La viuda honrada, su puerta cerrada.
The honest widow, behind a locked door.

El que se casa con viuda, rival tiene en otro mundo.
*The man who marries a widow has a rival in the
other world.*

La viuda llora y otros cantan en la boda.
At the wedding the widow cries as others sing.

*Viejo que boda
hace, requiescat
en pace.*

Old man who gets
married—may he
rest in peace.

FAMILY

LA FAMILIA

Sólo hay dos familias en este mundo,
los que tienen y los que no.
— Cervantes, *Don Quixote*
There are only two families in this world,
the haves and the have-nots.

No niega la cruz de su parroquia.
He doesn't deny the cross of his parish.
(He doesn't deny origins or family.)

Hijos no tenemos y nombres les ponemos.
Though we have no children, yet we give them names.

Hijo eres y padre serás.
Son you are and father you will be.

No hay más grande amor como el amor de madre.
There is no greater love than that of a mother.

Alaba la criatura y le haces amor a la madre.
Praise the child and you make love to the mother.

Ninguno diga quién es su padre sin que lo afirme la
madre.
No one knows his father except through his mother.

Sentirse la mamá de los pollitos.
Feeling like a mother hen.

Sentirse la mamá de Tarzán.
Feeling like Tarzan's mother.

Madre que consiente engorda una serpiente.
A mother who spoils feeds a serpent's coils.

De buena fuente, buena corriente.
From a good spring, a good current.

El árbol se conoce por su fruto.
A tree is known by its fruit.

Árbol que nace torcido, no se puede enderezar.
A tree that is born crooked can never be straightened.

*Amor de padre o
madre, que lo
demás es aire.*

Love of father and
mother, the rest is
pure air.

Parents & Children
Padres y niños

No dice la criatura sino lo que oye tras el fuego.

The child only repeats what she hears by the hearth.

El que con niños se acuesta, amanece mojado.
Who sleeps with children wakes up wet.

Hijos crecidos, trabajos llovidos.
When children grow up, troubles rain down.

De tal jarro, tal tecalpate.
A chip off the pot.

Hijo de bien, todos lo ven.
A well-mannered kid will never be hid.

Lo que con tus padres hicieres, tus hijos harán contigo.
What you do to your parents, your children will do to you.

Deje que el niño crezca y él dirá quién es su padre.
Let the child grow and he will say who his father is.

De tal palo, tal astilla.
From like stick, like sliver.
(*Like parent, like offspring.*)

El muchacho malcriado dondequiera encuentra padre.
An ill-bred child finds a father everywhere.

El hijo ausente no ve la muerte de su padre.
The absent son does not see the death of his father.

Sobre padre no hay compadre.
A compadre does not replace a father.

Hijo de gata, come ratón.
Hijo de gata, ratones mata.
The child of a cat will eat a rat.

El que quiera un hijo pillo, que lo meta de monaguillo.
If you want a naughty sprite, make your boy an acolyte.

Padre, mercader; hijo, caballero; nieto, pordiosero.
Father, merchant; son, gentleman; grandson, beggar.

El buen padre en la casa comienza.
A good parent begins at home.

De padre cojo, hijo rengo.
Lame father, crippled son.

De padre santo, hijo diablo.
Saintly father, devilish son.

El pan ajeno hace al hijo bueno.
Bread from next door makes a boy good to the core.

Hijo malo, más vale doliente que sano.
Bad son, better ill than well.

Parents &
Children
*Padres y
niños*

*Si a tu hijo no
le das castigo,
será tu peor
enemigo.*

If you do not
punish your
son, he will be
your worst
enemy.

*Donde hay hijos,
ni parientes ni
amigos.*

When children
are concerned,
neither relatives
nor friends
have a say.

Los padres que quieren a sus hijos, con más vara
los corrigen.
*Parents who love their children correct them more
earnestly.*

Cuando la vaca es ligera, la ternera va adelante.
When the cow is swift, the calf runs before her.
(The child will outpace the parents.)

Para que la cuña apriete, ha de ser del mismo palo.
*For the wedge of wood to fit tightly, it has to be from
the same block of wood.*
(The offense of brother, sister, or parents hurts more.)

A quien Dios no le da hijos, el Diablo le da sobrinos.
*To whom God gives no children, the devil gives nieces
and nephews.*

Un padre para cien hijos, no cien hijos para un padre.
*One father for a hundred children, not a hundred
children for one father.*

No hay peor astilla que la de la misma madera.
There is no worse sliver than that from the same wood.
(Relatives cause the worst pain.)

Vale más gota de sangre que arroba de amistad.
A drop of blood is worth more than a gallon of friendship.

Relatives
Parientes

Cuando los abuelos entran por la puerta, la disciplina sale por la ventana.
When grandparents come through the door, discipline goes out the window.

Niñas criadas con abuelas, nunca buenas.
Girls raised by their grandmothers are never good.

En casa de tía, pero no cada día.
See your aunt now and again, but every day would be a sin.

A mí no me digan tío, porque ni parientes somos.
Don't call me uncle—we're not even related.

Hermanos y gatos, todos son ingratos.
Relatives and cats are both ungrateful.

Más vale amigos cerca que parientes lejos.
It is better to have close friends than distant relatives.

De los parientes y el sol, entre más lejos mejor.
Relatives and the sun: The farther away the better.

Más cerca están mis dientes que mis parientes.
My teeth are closer than my relatives.

Parientes y trastes viejos, pocos y lejos.
Relatives, like old wine: few and far between.

Éramos pocos y parió mi abuela.

There were only a few of us when my grandmother had a baby.

(It's getting too crowded here.)

In-Laws
Suegros

La suegra no se acuerda que una vez fue nuera.

The mother-in-law doesn't remember she was once a daughter-in-law.

Suegro y yerno, ni en el infierno.
Father-in-law and son-in-law: not even in hell.

La mejor suegra, vestida de negro.
The best mother-in-law, dressed in black.

Aquél es bien casado, sin suegra, ni cuñada.
A man is well married who has neither a mother-in-law nor a sister-in-law.

Aquella es bien casada, sin suegra ni cuñada.
A woman is well married who has neither a mother-in-law nor a sister-in-law.

Los enemigos del hombre pueden ser la suegra, la cuñada y la mujer.
The enemies of a man may be the mother-in-law, the sister-in-law, or the wife.

Las suegras ni de azúcar son buenas.
Even the mothers-in-law made of sugar are no good.

Home
Hogar

Más sabe el loco en su casa que el cuerdo en la ajena.
The fool knows more in his own home than the wise person knows in his neighbor's.

En casa llena, pronto se guisa la cena.
In a full house, dinner will soon be ready.

En casa llena, pronto se cena.
In a full house, everyone eats right away.

¿A dónde vas que valgas más?
Where are you going that you are worth more?
(You're better off at home.)

Cada uno en su casa y Dios en la de todos.
Everyone in his house and God in everyone's.

Cuando veas tu casa quemar, acércate a calentar.
When you see your house begin to burn,
just draw close and get yourself warm.
(Take advantage of a bad situation.)

Casa con dos puertas, mala es de guardar.
A house with two doors is hard to defend.

Mi casa es chica pero es mi casa.
My house is small but it is my house.

Echar la casa por la ventana.
To throw the house out the window.

El que de su casa se aleja, no la encuentra como la deja.

Whoever leaves the house to roam, returns to find a different home.

Hospitality
Hospitalidad

El pan partido,
Dios aumenta.

Bread that is
shared, God
doubles.

Baile y cochino, en la casa del vecino.
Dancing and messes, in your neighbor's house.

De afuera vendrá el que de tu casa te echará.
From outside will come the one who will throw you
outside of your house.

De la casa ajena, el bocado más sabroso.
In someone else's house, the most delicious mouthful.

El que a tu casa no va, en la suya no te quiere.
If they won't come to your house, they don't want you
in theirs.

Bienvenidos los huéspedes por el gusto que dan cuando
se van.
Welcome, guests, for the joy you give us when you leave.

El huésped y el pez a los tres días apestan.
Guests and fish stink after three days.
    —Benjamin Franklin, *Poor Richard's Almanac*

De rincón a rincón, todo es colchón.
From one corner to another, it's all a mattress.

Vienes a deseo, hueles a poleo.
Come at your bent, you will smell of mint.
(You are welcome any time.)

Hospitality
Hospitalidad

Quien parte y comparte se queda con la mejor parte.
The one who divies into parts ends up with the better part.

El que reparte y comparte
y al repartir tiene tino
siempre deja de contino
para sí la mejor parte.
The one who divies into parts—
the one who has that knack—
always holds a little back,
and so ends up with the better part.

El que come y no da ¿qué corazón tendrá?
Who eats without sharing, what kind of heart must
they have?

El día que no escobí, vino quien no pensé.
The day I didn't sweep, an unexpected visitor came.

De las nueve en adelante no hay visita que se aguante.

From nine o'clock on, all guests should be gone.

FRIENDS & NEIGHBORS

LOS AMIGOS Y LOS VECINOS

Una no es ninguna.
One is not none.

Dos es compañía pero tres es nada.
Two is company but three is none.

Buenas son mis vecinas pero me faltan tres gallinas.
My neighbors are good, but I'm missing three chickens.

A cada cual con lo suyo.
To each his own.

Que todos sean tus amigos y en particular ninguno.
May all be your friends and no one in particular.

Muchos los amigos y pocos los escogidos.
Muchos son los amigos pero poco los escogidos.
Make many friends, but choose only a few.

Muchos conocidos, pocos amigos.
Many acquaintances, few friends.

Dime con quién andas y te diré quién eres.
Tell me who your friends are and I will tell you who you are.

Más vale solo que mal acompañado.
Better alone than in bad company.

Vida sin amigos, muerte sin testigos.
Life without friends: No mourners when it ends.

Se escoge bien al amigo, más no al hermano ni al hijo.
*You can choose your friends but not your sibling or
your child.*

Compañero ingenioso, hace el camino corto.
An amusing companion makes the journey shorter.

Juntos pero no revueltos.
Together but not mixed.

*Amigo cabal,
tesoro ideal.*

True friend,
ideal treasure.

Friends & Foes

Amigos y enemigos

Al buen amigo con tu pan y con tu vino, y al malo con tu perro y con tu palo.

Bread and your wine for your good friend, your dog and a stick for your bad friend.

Las piedras rodando se encuentran.
Rolling stones will eventually meet.
(*This is a small world.*)

Mientras al cielo no subas, nos veremos.
As long as you don't go to heaven, we will meet again.

Los amigos de mis amigos son mis amigos.
Any friend of yours is a friend of mine.

El amigo y el vino, antiguos.
With friends and wines, the older the better.

A buen árbol te arrimas.
You are getting close to a good tree.
(*You are getting close to a friend.*)

El que a buen árbol se arrima, buena sombra le cobija.
When you get close enough to a good tree, you find a welcome shade.

Entre más amistad, más claridad.
The deeper the friendship, the deeper the understanding.

Más vale malo por conocido que bueno por conocer.
Better a bad person you know than a good one you don't.

Mis amigos no alzan la pata para mear.
My friends don't raise their legs to pee.
(*My friends are not dogs.*)

Amigo viejo, el mejor espejo.
An old friend is the best mirror.

Entre amigos honrados, cumplimientos dispensados.
Among good friends, formalities shall end.

Las amistades no se han de romper, sino descoser.
Friendships should not be broken, but rather unsewn.

Al amigo y al caballo, no apretallo, o no cansallo.
Never worry or tire your friend or your horse.

Al amigo y al caballo no cansarlos.
Tire neither your friend nor your horse.

Intimidad cría desprecio.
Familiarity breeds contempt.

Mírote a deseo, hueles a poleo; mírote cada rato, hueles
a chivato.
*If I see you when I want to, you smell like mint; when I see
you all the time, you smell like a goat.*

Olla que mucho hierve, sabor pierde.
A pot that boils too much loses flavor.
(Familiarity breeds contempt.)

No te fíes de amigo reconciliado, ni de manjar dos
veces guisado.
Do not trust a reconciled friend nor a dish twice cooked.

*El amigo impru-
dente, de una
piedra mata una
mosca en la
frente.*

An imprudent
friend would kill
a fly on your
forehead with
a stone.

Friends & Foes
Amigos y enemigos

Amistad que siempre dice "dame," más que amistad, parece hambre.

A friendship that always says "give me" looks less like friendship, more like hunger.

Amigo en la adversidad, amigo de realidad.
A friend in need is a friend indeed.

En la cárcel y en la cama se conocen los amigos.
In jail and in bed you learn who are your friends.

En el peligro se conoce al amigo.
When in danger, you get to know your friend.

Amigo que no da y cuchillo que no corta, que se pierdan, no importan.
A friend who will not give and a knife that will not cut—lose them, they aren't needed.

Amigos que pelean sobre pedazo de pan centeno, o el hambre es grande o el amor es pequeño.
*When, for a bit of rye bread, friends will fight,
either their hunger is great or their love is slight.*

En tiempos de higos, no hay amigos.
When fig-picking time comes around, there are never friends to be found.

El amigo de buenos tiempos múdase con el viento.
A good-time friend sways with the wind.

Al decir las verdades se pierden las amistades.
In telling the truth, friendships are lost.

Friends & Foes

Amigos y enemigos

Una cosa es la amistad, otra cosa es, "¡no la friegues!"
Friendship is one thing, another is—"You're overdoing it!"

Cuando se enojan las comadres, salen las verdades.
When good women friends fall out, the truth comes to light.

Compadre que a la comadre no le anda por las caderas,
no es amigo de veras.
*A best friend who does not make passes at one's wife is not
a good friend.*
(A cynical comment.)

El más amigo es traidor y el más verdadero miente.
Best friends will betray and the most honest will lie.

La lengua del mal amigo más corta que el cuchillo.
The tongue of a false friend is sharper than a knife.

Son tres los únicos amigos fieles: la esposa vieja, el perro
y el dinero.
*There are but three true friends: an old wife, a dog,
and money.*

Más ven cuatro ojos que dos.
Four eyes can see better than two.

La amistad vale más que el dinero.
Friendship is worth more than money.

*Vale mas onza de
amistad que libra
de hostilidad.*

Better an ounce
of friendship
than a pound
of hostility.

*No hay enemigo
chico.*

*No hay enemigo
pequeño.*

There is
no small
enemy.

La amistad es una cosa y el negocio otra.
Friendship is one thing and business another.

Al platicar, como amigos; al tratar, como enemigos.
Converse like friends; negotiate like enemies.

Entre dos amigos, un notario y dos testigos.
*Business between friends requires a coterie:
two witnesses as well as a notary.*

Si a tu amigo quieres probar, finge necesidad.
If you want to put your friend to a test, feign need.

Guárdate del amigo que alterna con tu enemigo.
Be wary of a friend who associates with your enemy.

No todas las cosas se han de apurar, ni todos los amigos
probar, ni todos los enemigos decubrir y declarar.
*Not all things should be hurried, not all friends tested,
not all enemies discovered and declared.*

La envidia del amigo es peor que el odio del enemigo.
The envy of a friend is worse than the hatred of the enemy.

Trata con el enemigo, como si en breve haya de ser amigo
o con el amigo, si hubiese de ser enemigo.
*Treat the enemy as if he will soon be your friend;
and the friend as if he will soon be your enemy.*

Friends & Foes
Amigos y enemigos

Ni le vendas a tu amigo, ni le compres a tu enemigo.
Don't sell to your friends, nor buy from your enemy.

No hay más amigo que Dios ni más pariente que un peso.
There is no better friend than God nor closer relative than the peso.
(*Trust in God, all others pay cash.*)

Amigo reconciliado, enemigo agazapado.
A reconciled friend is an enemy in ambush.

No me defiendas, compadre.
Don't defend me, good friend.
(*With friends like you who needs enemies?*)

Con amigos como tú, no hacen falta los enemigos.
With friends like you, who needs enemies?

Bueno para amigo, malo para enemigo.
Good as a friend, bad as an enemy.
(*Choose your friends and enemies carefully.*)

Del enemigo te librarás, pero del mal amigo, jamás.
From the enemy you will liberate yourself, but from a bad friend, never.

Ni en el peor enemigo hay que perder fe.
Not even with your worst enemy should you lose faith.

Al amigo, sin razón; al enemigo ni con ella.

A friend does not have to be right; for an enemy even being right is not enough.

Friends & Foes
Amigos y enemigos

Elogio de enemigos es oro fino.

The highest possible praise is that which comes from our enemies.

Cien amigos son pocos; y un enemigo es mucho.
One hundred friends are not enough; one enemy is too many.

Viene a ti el enemigo humillado, guárdate de él como del diablo.
When your enemy approaches you humbly, guard yourself as from the devil.

Al enemigo que huye, puente de plata.
To a fleeing enemy, a silver bridge.
(Help the enemy retreat: Don't kick a a person when he's down.)

Nunca falta un pelo en la sopa.
There's always a hair in the soup.
(There's one in every crowd.)

Una mano lava la otra y las dos lavan la cara.
One hand washes the other, and the two together
wash the face.

Favor ofrecido,
compromiso
contraído.

Favor offered,
obligation
contracted.

El favor recibido debe ser correspondido.
If you take a favor, return it later.

El dinero se paga, pero el favor no.
Money can be repaid, but a favor cannot.

Favor publicado, favor deshonrado.
A favor made public is without honor.

Favor con anuncio, ni lo busco ni lo quiero.
El favor con pregonero, ni lo pido ni lo quiero.
A favor that is announced, I neither ask for nor want.

Favor referido, ni de Dios ni del diablo agradecido.
A spoken favor pleases neither God nor the devil.

Agua le pido a mi Dios y a los aguadores nada.
Water I ask from my God, but from the water
carriers nothing.
(I ask favors from no one.)

El que le lava la cara al burro, pierde su tiempo y pierde
el jabón.
Who washes a burro's face wastes time and soap.
(Not everybody appreciates your favors.)

Help
Ayuda

*Mucha ayuda,
poco trabajo.*

Many hands
make light
work.

Un burro rasca a otro.
One burro scratches another.

La ayuda llega de quien menos la espera.
Help comes from where you least expect it.
(*Even the humblest friend can be of great help.*
   —Aesop's *The Lion and the Mouse*)

Ahora verás, huarache, ya apareció tu correa.
Look, sandal, your strap has just appeared.

Anda tu camino, sin ayuda del vecino.
Follow your own way, without your neighbor's aid.

Quien siembra en tierra ajena, hasta la semilla pierde.
Who sows on a neighbor's land will lose even the seed.

Dios da pañuelo al que no tiene nariz.
God gives a handkerchief to those who have no nose.

La casada le pide a la viuda.
The married woman beseeches the widow.
(*Asking help from someone who needs more help than you.*)

Unos de pedir se cansan y otros sin pedir les dan.
*Some wear themselves out from asking; others receive
without asking.*

Como arco iris, siempre sales después de la tempestad.
Like a rainbow, you always come out after the storm.

Help
Ayuda

A lo dado no se le busca lado.
Given a gift, don't question the drift.

A caballo regalado, no se le ve diente.
Don't look a gift horse in the mouth.

Por pedir, nada se pierde.
You lose nothing by asking.

El pedir es fuerza, dar es voluntad.
To ask is strength, to give is will.

Sí ofrecer, pero no dar.
Offer yes, but give no.

Más vale comprado que regalado.
Better bought than given.

El que por otro pide, por si aboga.
In asking for another, you are pleading for yourself.

Quien pide poco, nada merece.
Who asks for little deserves nothing.

Al que hace más se le agradece menos.
The one who does the most is thanked the least.

Mucho ayuda el que poco estorba.
Harto ayuda el que no estorba.
The one who interferes the least helps the most.

En el modo de pedir está el modo de dar.

In the manner of asking is the manner of giving.

Talk
Conversación

Haz bien a los presentes y habla bien de los ausentes.

Do good to those present and speak well of those absent.

La buena educación conviene, para usarla con quien la tiene.
Good manners are handy if you come upon good-mannered folk to use them on.

La cortesía de boca gana mucho a poco costo.
Courteous words gain much at little cost.

Cortesía de boca mucho consigue y nada cuesta.
Courteous words attain much and cost nothing.

Lo cortés no quita lo valiente.
Courtesy doesn't take away from valor.

El más lento en prometer es siempre el más seguro en cumplir.
The slower one to promise is always the most sure to comply.

Dicho y hecho.
Said and done.

Una cosa es prometer, otra cosa es cumplir.
One thing is to promise, another is to fulfill your word.

En la boca del descreto, lo público es secreto.
If one is discreet, news won't hit the street.
(In the mouth of the discreet, public information is secret.)

Vale más decir que harán que decir que haré.
It's better to say what they'll do than to say what you'll do.

Palabra y piedra suelta, no tienen vuelta.
Words and a rolling stone never come back.

No hay burla tan leve, que aguijón no lleve.
There's no teasing so slight that it doesn't leave a little bite.

¡Sangre de venado! Todo lo que digas se irá para'l lado.
Blood of a deer! Everything you say will fall by the wayside.

Si dudas, calla o pregunta.
If you are in doubt, either be quiet or ask.

En la duda, abstente.
When in doubt, abstain.

Más vale callar que mal hablar.
Better to remain silent than to speak badly.

Ni todo lo que sepas digas, ni todo lo que tengas da.
Don't say everything you know nor everything you have.

Ni veas mal todo lo viejo, ni alabes todo lo nuevo.
Don't despise all the old nor praise all the new.

Se dice el pecado pero no el pecador.
Name the sin but not the sinner.
(Don't mention any names.)

El Fray Modesto nunca llegó a prior.
Friar Modest never became prior.

Quien pregunta lo que no debe, le responden lo que no quiere.

If your question is out of bounds, you won't like how the answer sounds.

(Use a little tact.)

EN POCAS
PALABRAS

Talk
Conversación

Buen abogado, mal vecino.

Good lawyer, bad neighbor.

(Nosy neighbors, bad friends.)

En casa del ahorcado no se ha de nombrar la soga.
In the hanged man's house never mention the noose.
(*Don't rub it in; Don't bring up the past.*)

Nunca preguntes lo que no te importa.
Never ask what is none of your business.

En boca cerrada no entran moscas.
Flies do not enter a closed mouth.

Cuida tu casa y deja la ajena.
Take care of your house and leave your neighbor's alone.

Come camote, no te dé pena, cuida tu casa y deja la ajena.
To eat sweet potatoes never be ashamed—care for your house, from your neighbor's abstain.
(*Camotes cause gas.*)

El que tiene tejado de vidrio que no tire pidras al de su vecino.
People with glass roofs should not throw rocks at their neighbor's house.

Cada perico a su mecate y cada chango a su metate.
Every parrot to its perch and every monkey to its task.
(*Mind your own business.*)

Si quieres que sepan lo que eres, cuéntaselo a las mujeres.
If you want people to know who you are, just tell the women, and the word will go far.

Cae más pronto un hablador que un cojo.
A loudmouth falls quicker than a cripple does.

El que mucho habla mucho yerra.
Who talks much, errs much.

Gossiping
and lying go
together.

No todo lo que dice el panadero es cierto.
Not everything the baker says is true.

El Diablo estando ocioso, se metió de chismoso.
The devil, finding himself idle, began to gossip.

El chisme agrada, el chismoso enfada.
Gossip one enjoys; the gossiper annoys.

Chisme averiguado jamás es acabado.
Gossip once begun will never be done.

La envidia es madre del chisme.
Envy is the mother of gossip.

La ropa sucia se lava en casa.
Dirty linen is washed at home.

De aquellos polvos vienen estos lodos.
From that dust comes this mud.
(Past sins have a way of catching up.)

No hay duda que la basura flota.
There is no doubt—garbage floats.

Talk
Conversación

*Las maldiciones
caen sobre quien
las dice.*

Curses fall on
whoever wishes
them.

(Curses come
home to
roost.)

Quien te traiga un cuento, despídelo al momento.
Whoever has a story to tell, quickly bid that person farewell.

El que escucha, mierda embucha.
Who eavesdrops eats shit.

Quien tiene rabo de paja no debe acercarse al fuego.
People who have a straw tail should not get close to the fire.
(People who live in glass houses shouldn't throw stones.)

De los escarmentados nacen los avisados.
From the punished are born the forewarned.

Aunque frío y callado, predica bien el ahorcado.
Although cold and silent, the hanged preach well.

Los que viven por la espalda, por la espalda morirán.
Those who live behind the back, will die behind the back.

No hay provocativo que salga con bien.
There is no provocation that comes out well.

De lo que veas cree muy poco; de lo que te cuentan, nada.
Of what you see, believe little; of what they tell you, nothing.

Donde lumbre ha habido, rescoldo queda.
Where a fire has burnt, an ember remains.

Donde no hay humo, no hay lumbre.
Where there is no smoke, there is no fire.

Talk
Conversación

Ya se descubrió el pastel.
The pie has been discovered.
(*The cat's out of the bag.*)

Donde quitan y no ponen, descomponen.
If you take and don't restore, things will fall apart for sure.

Nunca digas que llueve hasta que truene.
Never say it's raining until you hear thunder.
(*Never cry "Wolf!" until you see one.*)

Quien es ruin en su aldea, ruin será dondequiera.
A person despised in his own village is despised everywhere.

Cuando el sartén chilla, algo hay en la villa.
When the frying pan sounds, something's happening in town.

Las paredes tienen oídos.
The walls have ears.

De un cuento nacen cien.
From one story, a hundred are born.

Cuando el río suena, agua lleva.
In a babbling brook, water is rushing.
(*Rumors often have an element of truth.*)

Cuando el río suena, piedras lleva.
A babbling brook is carrying stones.

Pueblo chico, infierno grande.

Small town, large hell.

(Everyone knows everyone and everybody's business.)

EN POCAS
PALABRAS

Talk
Conversación

*La mala llaga
sana, la mala
fama mata.*

A bad wound
heals, bad
reputation
kills.

Cuando se seca el arroyo, se sabe lo que llevaba.
When the stream runs dry, you know what it carried.
(*Once you're known, you can deceive no one.*)

Nadie diga de sí nada, que sus obras lo dirán.
Nobody speaks for himself—his words speak for him.

El nombre dura más que la persona.
The name lasts longer than the person.

A quien mala fama tiene, ni acompañes ni quieras bien.
*Don't accompany nor love dearly one who has a bad
reputation.*

Por una vez que maté a un perro, me llamaron mataperros.
Because I once killed a dog, they call me a dog killer.

A quien dices tus secretos, das tu libertad y estás sujeto.
*The one you tell your secrets to, you cede your freedom
and are subject to.*

Tu secreto dijiste, esclavo te hiciste.
Your secret you gave, now you're a slave.

Secreto en reunión es de mala educación.
Telling secrets in gatherings is low class.

Un secreto entre dos ya no es secreto.
A secret shared with another is no longer a secret.

Talk
Conversación

Secreto de tres, secreto que no es.
A secret among three can no secret be.

Secreto de muchos, secreto de nadie.
Secret among many, secret to none.

Secreto de dos, secreto de Dios; secreto de tres,
secreto del diablo.
A secret between two is God's; a secret among three
is the devil's.

Secreto entre dos completo si uno está muerto.
A secret between two is complete if one is dead.

Pecado callado, medio perdonado.
A sin that's hidden is half forgiven.

Filo de hacha corta pino, no hocico de coyotino.
The sharp edge of an axe cuts the pine tree,
not the mouth of a coyote.
(Actions speak louder than words.)

Si no quieres que
tu amigo tenga el
pie sobre tu
pescuezo, no le
descubras tus
secretos.

If you don't want
your friend's foot
on your neck,
don't let him
in on your
secrets.

Friendly Relations
Buenas relaciones

Consejo es de sabios, perdonar injurias y olvidar agravios.

Advice from the wise for getting along: Forgive insults and forget past wrongs.

En pleito claro, no es menester letrado.
In an altercation you don't need education.

Sobre cuernos penitencia.
Insult on top of injury.
(*Adding salt to the wound.*)

Con una brasa se quema la casa.
It takes a single cinder to turn a house to tinder.
(*It only takes a word to start an argument.*)

De las burlas pesadas, se llegan a puñaladas.
Cutting jibes will lead to knives.

Dar bofetada con guante blanco.
Slapping with a white glove.

El que pega primero, pega dos veces.
Who hits first, hits twice.

Tirar la piedra y esconder la mano.
He throws the rock and hides his hand.

Cuando uno no quiere, dos no pelean.
When one doesn't want to, the two won't fight.
(*It takes two to tangle.*)

No es defecto correr cuando se iguala la pelea.
It is no defect to run when the fight is even.

Quien no oye más que una campana, no oye más que un sonido.
Who hears but one bell, hears but one sound.
(There are two sides to any argument.)

Satisfacción no pedida, acusación manifiesta.
Apology not asked for, guilt confirmed.

El que no perdona a su enemigo no tiene a Dios por su amigo.
El que perdona a su enemigo, a Dios tiene por amigo.
Who pardons his foe, with God will go.

El perdón, si es retrasado, no lo goza el perdonado.
Forgiveness that's late carries little weight.

Errar es humano, perdonar es divino.
To err is human, to forgive is divine.
　　—Alexander Pope, *Essay on Criticism*

Perdonar es valentía, no perdonar es cobardía.
To forgive is courage, not to forgive is cowardice.

El perdón es la forma divina de amar.
Forgiveness is the divine form of love.

No juzguen a otros, para que Dios no los juzgue a ustedes.
Judge not, that ye shall not be judged.
　　—Old Testament, Matthew VII, 1

Friendly Relations
Buenas relaciones

El que vivió de ilusiones no alcanza el perdón de Dios.

Who lived a life of illusions will not obtain God's forgiveness.

Friendly
Relations
Buenas
relaciones

Ni quito ni pongo rey.

I neither remove nor name kings.

(I will take no part in this.)

A mí me corresponde hacer justicia.
Vengeance is mine.
        —New Testament, Romans, XII, 19–20

No debes juzgar sin antes verte juzgado.
Judge yourself before you judge others.

Ni absuelvas ni condenes, si cabal noticia no tienes.
Neither absolve nor reprimand, unless you have the facts in hand.

El buen juez por su casa empieza.
The good judge begins at home.

Por un borrego no se juzga la manada.
Don't judge the whole flock by a single sheep.

De juez de poca conciencia, no esperes justa sentencia.
From a judge with little conscience, don't expect a just sentence.

El peor testigo es tu amigo.
The worst testimony is that of your friend.

Más poderoso es el ruego del amigo que el fierro del enemigo.
A friend's entreaty is more powerful than the sword of the enemy.

Friendly Relations
Buenas relaciones

De un ladrón me guardo, pero no de un testimonio falso.
I can defend myself against a thief, but not against false testimony.

Juicio precipitado es casi siempre errado.
A kangaroo court always falls short.

Para ser justo, hasta con el Diablo.
To be just, give the devil his due.

Échale tierra al pasado.
Bury the past.
(*Let bygones be bygones.*)

Haz y deja hacer a los demás.
Do, and allow others to do.
(*Live and let live.*)

No es boda sino un humilde baile familiar.
It's not a wedding but a humble family party.
(*Sorry, you have the wrong house.*)

El que nace para maceta del corredor no pasa.
Who was born to be a flowerpot will never leave the hallway.
(*A hint to move.*)

Justicia sin benigdad no es justicia sino crueldad.

Justice that is not benign is not justice but cruelty.

POLITICS

❖

POLÍTICA

Uno para todos y todos para uno.
All for one and one for all.

El pueblo unido, jamás será vencido.
A people united will never be defeated.

O todos hijos o todos entenados.
Either we are all children or all step-children.

No me veas de la cumbre al valle, que estamos a la misma altura.
Don't look at me as from the summit to the valley; we are at the same altitude.

No están todos los que son, ni son todos los que están.
Not everyone is here, and those who are here aren't everyone.
(Some who are here are not really here;
or, some who are here really do not belong.)

Es del otro cachete.
A person from the other cheek.
(A person from Mexico.)

Government
Gobierno

No me digas del partido de paz ni del partido de guerra;
es lo mismo que me muerda un perro que una perra.
Don't tell me about the party of peace or the party of war;
it's the same whether a male or female dog bites me.

El que es ciego de nación, nunca sabe por dónde anda.
Who is blind to his own nation will never know where
he is traveling.

Las cosas de palacio siempre van despacio.
A palace's ways can stretch on for days.
(The ways of the government are always slow.)

Voz del pueblo, sube al cielo.
Clamor del pueblo sube al cielo.
The outcry of a people rises to heaven.

Voz del pueblo, voz del cielo.
Voice of the people, voice of heaven.

Pueblo dividido, pueblo vencido.
A people divided, a people conquered.

Cada uno jala pa' su lado.
Everyone pulls toward his own side.
(Everyone looks after his own interests.)

Donde manda capitán, no ordena marinero.
Where the captain commands, the sailor doesn't
give orders.

*El que hizo la
ley, hizo la
trampa.*

Whoever made
the law made
the trap.

Authority
Autoridad

El amo imprudente hace al mozo negligente.

A careless master makes negligent servants.

Pides levantón y quieres manejar.
You ask for a lift and you want to drive.

Para saber mandar, es preciso saber obedecer.
To know how to give orders one must know how to obey.

En el trono, sólo cabe un culo.
On the throne there is room for only one asshole.

Va el rey donde puede y no donde quiere.
The king goes where he can, not where he wants.

El perro le manda al gato, y el gato a su cola.
The dog bosses the cat and the cat bosses its tail.

Manda, haz, y serás bien servido.
Command, then do it yourself, and you will be well served.
(If you want things done, do them yourself.)

Con virtud y bondad, se adquiere autoridad.
With virtue and goodness, one acquires authority.

Cual el amo, tal el criado.
As master, as servant.
(Set good examples.)

Cuando la fuerza ríe, la razón llora.
When force laughs, reason cries.

Power
Poder

La desgracia es la cruda del poder.
Disgrace is power's hangover.

Querer es poder.
Desire is power.

Al más potente, cede el más prudente.
The prudent yield to the powerful.

Poder corrumpe.
Power corrupts.

Más vale maña que fuerza.
Better brains than brawn.

Al haber gatos, no hay ratones.
Where there are cats, there are no mice.
(Where there is strength, there is no opposition.)

Más vale maña que fuerza.
Skill is better than strength.

Donde hay aguilillas, no cuentan gavilanes.
Where there are eagles, hawks don't count.
(The spoils belong to the strong.)

A fuerza, ni los zapatos entran.
By force, not even shoes fit.
(Nothing is gained by force.)

El poder manda.

Power commands.

(Might is right.
—Plato, *The
Republic* I)

History
Historia

*Felices los pueblos
cuya historia es
aburrida.*

Happy are the
people whose
history is
boring.

A la guerra con la guerra.
Fight war with war.
(*Fight fire with fire.*)

El que tonto va a la guerra, tonto regresa de ella.
Who leaves for war as a fool, as a fool returns.
(*There is nothing to be learned from war.*)

Señas en el cielo, guerra en el suelo.
Signs in the sky, war on the ground.

Vale más una cierta paz que una victoria dudosa.
It's better to have certain peace than uncertain victory.

Quien quiera la paz, que aprenda a pelear.
Who wants peace must first learn to fight.

Lo peor de los pleitos es que de uno nacen cientos.
The worst thing about fights is that one breeds hundreds.

Cuesta poquito más vivir en paz.
It costs little more to live in peace.

El pueblo que pierde su historia, pierde su destino.
A people who lose their history lose their destiny.

La ley de Caifás: al amolado, amolarlo más.
The law of Caliphs: The downtrodden, trample some more.

BUSINESS DEALINGS

NEGOCIOS

Diligencia es madre de la industria.
Diligence is the mother of industry.

Los premios del trabajo justo son honra, provecho y gusto.
Rewards for honest labor are honor, good health, and joy.

La mierda, entre más le escarban, mas jiede.
The more you sift the shit, the worse it smells.
(The more you look into a shady deal, the stinkier it gets.)

Entre menos burros, más elotes.
The fewer donkeys, the more corn.

Arrear que vienen arreando.
Keep things moving.

Business
Comercio

Vale más un mal acuerdo que un buen pleito.

Better a bad agreement than a good fight.

Más vale doblarse que quebrarse.
Better to bend than to break.

Más vale mala agencia que buena sentencia.
Better a poor agreement than a good lawsuit.

Con los curas y los gatos, pocos tratos.
There are few contracts with curates and cats.

El peor de los males es tratar con animales.
The worst evil is to deal with beasts.

Negocio que no deja, dejarlo.
A business that does not leave you anything should be left.

Da más y recibirás menos.
Give more and you will receive less.

Negocio platicado, negocio no arreglado.
Business disputed is not executed.

Ese arroz ya se coció.
That rice is cooked.
(When a business deal is done.)

Buenas cuentas, buenos amigos.
Good accounts, good friends.

Unas de cal por unas de arena.
A bit of lime for a bit of sand.

Si doy, más que tonto soy,
si fío, pierdo lo que no es mío;
si presto, me hacen mal gesto,
por lo tanto desde hoy,
para ahorrarme de este lío
ni doy, ni fío, ni presto.
If I give things away, then I'm worse than a fool.
But selling on credit, what I lose is not even mine;
And if I lend, people will treat me like swine.
So I resolve, beginning today,
from this problem to get away,
and not to give, sell on credit, nor lend will be my rule.

*Cuesta caro
tirar maíz a las
palomas por la
codicia de pillar
un pichón.*

It's expensive
to cast maize to
the doves hoping
to catch one
pigeon.

Más vale renta que venta.
To rent well is better than to sell.

El que no enseña, no vende.
If you do not display, you will not sell.

Vender la piel del oso antes de cazarlo.
Selling the skin before hunting the bear.

El que paga manda.
Who pays, commands.
(The customer is always right.)

Es más rico, el rico cuando empobrece; que el pobre
cuando enriquece.
*When the wealthy get poor they are still wealthier than even
the poor who get rich.*

Business
Comercio

*Primero la
obligación, que
la devoción.*

First duty, then
devotion.

(Business before
pleasure.)

No perder es ganancia.
Not to lose is to profit.

El que fía salió a cobrar.
The person who sells on credit went out to collect.
(*Polite formula, often a sign, meaning: "The person who
gives credit is out of the store."*)

El que tiene tienda, que la atienda, o si no, que la venda.
*If you have a shop, there you must stop; but if you can't
make it your personal workshop, then shop it around.*

¡Averígualo, Vargas!
Find out, Vargas!
(*What Queen Isabella's magistrate, Don Fernando Vargas,
was told on various occasions.*)

El que no fía, no vende.
Who does not sell on credit, does not sell.

El que regala, bien vende si el que lo recibe lo entiende.
A gift will soon with a sale repay, if taken in the right way.
(*Gifts are good investments.*)

Lo fiado es pariente de lo dado.
Credit is the cousin of the gift.

A la feria muchos van, a ver y no a comprar.
Many go to the fair to browse and not to buy.

El que quiera azul celeste, ¡que le cueste!
If you want a blue sky, the cost will be high.

El que quiera tener becerro, que compre vaca.
Who wants to own a calf should buy a cow.

El que manda no se equivoca y si se equivoca, que
vuelva a mandar.
*The one who orders never makes mistakes—or if he
does, he gives another order.*

Mira bien y con cuidado y en toda empresa
determinado.
*Look well and carefully and in all enterprises act with
determination.*

No comprará barato quien no ruega un rato.
*Unless you haggle more than a peep, you will never get
it cheap.*

Es más barato comprarlo que rogarlo.
It is cheaper to buy it than to beg for it.

Los que compran barato, compran cada rato.
*Those who buy when the cost is low will make a purchase
every time.*

La diligencia es madre de la buena ventura.
Diligence is the mother of a good undertaking.

*Abrir un agujero
para tapar otro.*

Dig one
hole to fill
another.

(Rob Peter to
pay Paul.)

Work
Trabajo

*El trabajo es
virtud.*

Work is a
virtue.

Sólo Dios sabe para quién trabajas.
Only God knows for whom you work.

Nadie sabe para quién trabaja.
Nadie sabe por quién trabaja.
No one knows for whom they work.
(*No one knows who benefits from the fruits of his labor.*)

A quien es trabajador, le pesa que se haga noche.
A good worker regrets the coming of night.

A quien de trabajos no sabe, poco afán se hace grave.
*If to work you're not accountable, the smallest task will
seem insurmountable.*

Al mal trabajador, no le viene bien ningún azadón.
To a bad worker, no tool works right.

Garañón que no relincha, que lo capen.
The stallion that does not neigh should be castrated.
(*Get rid of a worker who does not perform.*)

Antes trabajaba y ahora es trabajoso.
He used to work, now he's a lot of work.

Los criados son enemigos pagados.
Servants are paid enemies.

El trabajo es sagrado, no lo toques.
Work is sacred, don't touch it.

Ni pidas a quien pidió, ni sirvas a quien sirvió.
Ni sirvas a quien sirvió, ni pidas a quien pidió, ni mandes
a quien mandó, ni ames a quien amó.
Don't ask one who has asked, nor serve one who has served,
nor command one who has commanded, nor love one who
has loved.

El trabajo de los niños es poco y el que no lo aprovecha
es loco.
A child's work is little but anyone who fails to cultivate
it is crazy.

El trabajo no es entrar sino encontrar la salida.
Getting in isn't work but looking for the way out is.

No hay atajo sin trabajo.
There is no shortcut without work.

Andar buscando trabajo pidiendo a Dios no encontrarlo.
Looking for work and praying not to find it.

De que los hay, los hay; el trabajo es dar con ellos.
If they exist, they exist—the only trouble is finding them.

Los platicadores y los desocupados son el azote de los
ocupados.
Chatterers and the idle are the scourge of the industrious.

De bajada hasta las piedras ruedan.
Downhill, even rocks roll.

Mucho ruido,
poco trabajo.

Big noise,
little work.

Work
Trabajo

Aprendiz de todo, oficial de nada.

Apprentice of all, official of nothing.

(Jack of all trades, master of none.)

Nunca solicites comisión que no se te encomienda.
Never volunteer for anything.

Del trabajar nace el descansar.
Rest is born from work.

Si el ocio causa tedio, el trabajo es buen remedio.
If idleness causes boredom, work is a good remedy.

Trabajar como negros para vivir como blancos.
Work like Blacks to live like Whites.
(Or say slaves, Mexicans, Chinese, women, etc.)

El basurero no huele a su compañero.
Garbage collectors can't smell each other.

No todos los que chiflan son arrieros.
Not all whistlers are animal drivers.

Al que le ven caballo, le ofrecen silla.
Whoever looks like a horse will be offered a saddle.

Entre sastres no se pagan los remiendos.
Between tailors repairs are free.

En casa del jabonero, el que no cae, resbala.
In the soap maker's home if you don't fall, at least you slip.

En casa de herrero, cucharón de palo.
In the blacksmith's house, the big spoon is made of wood.

Work
Trabajo

En el modo de cortar el queso se conoce al que es tendero.
How the cheese is sliced tells you who the shopkeeper is.

De carrocero a perrero.
From chauffer to dog catcher.

Antes de cazar, tener casa en que morar y tierras que labrar.
Before going hunting, make sure you have a house to live in and land to toil.

Lo que de noche se hace, de día mal parece.
What is made by night, looks bad by day.

Tejado de un rato, labor para todo el año.
A temporary roof means year-around work.

Lo bien hecho ni trabajo da venderlo.
The well-made product isn't hard to sell.

Más vale una yunta andando que cien paradas.
A yoke of oxen is worth more than a hundred untethered.

El trabajo hace la vida agradable.
Work makes life more pleasant.

El trabajo ennoblece pero también envejece.
Work ennobles but it also ages.

Fierro movedizo no cría mojo.
A moving piece of iron never rusts.

El que primero va al molino, primero muele.

First to the mill, first to grind.

Money
Dinero

*El dinero no es
santo pero hace
milagros.*

Money is no saint
but it works
miracles.

El águila siendo animal se retrató en el dinero.
The eagle—only an animal—got engraved on money.
(Anyone can succeed.)

La primera mordida mexicana: el áquila con la serpiente
en el pico.
*The first Mexican bite (bribe): The eagle with the serpent
in its beak.*

¿Qué mis pesos no tienen águila?
Don't my pesos have an eagle?
(Isn't my money any good?)

Más ablanda el dinero que la palabra del caballero.
*For smoothing things over, better is money
than even a gentleman's words like honey.*

La gloria es de quien la gana y el dinero de quien
lo agarra.
*Glory belongs to he who earns it and money to he who
grabs it.*

El dinero es tan mal amo como buen criado.
Money is as bad a master as it is a good servant.

Armas y dinero, buenas manos requieren.
Weapons and money require good hands.

La ambición del dinero hace al hombre pecador.
Love of money makes a man a sinner.

Money
Dinero

No hay general que resista un cañonazo de cincuenta mil pesos.
No general can resist a salvo of fifty thousand pesos.

El amor al dinero es raíz de toda clase de males.
Love of money is the root of all evil.
    —New Testament, I Timothy, VI, 10

Lo que no es necesario, por ningún precio es barato.
What is not needed is expensive at any price.

Llave de oro abre cualquier puerta.
A gold key opens any door.

Cuida tus centavos, que tus pesos se cuidan solos.
Take care of your pennies and your dollars will take care of themselves.

Dos andares tiene el dinero: viene despacio y se va ligero.
Two walking styles has Mr. Cash: He comes in slowly and leaves in a flash.

Echarle dinero bueno al malo.
Throwing good money after bad.

Amigo de rico, peso en la bolsa.
The rich man's friend, money in the pocket.

Con plata, nada falta.
With money nothing will be lacking.

Poderoso caballero es don Dinero.

A powerful gentleman is Mr. Money.

Money
Dinero

Cuando el dinero habla, todos callan.

When money speaks, everyone becomes silent.

A dineros pagados, brazos quebrados.
Money paid out, workers laid up.
(*Don't pay for work before it's done.*)

Dinero llama dinero.
Money makes money.

El dinero todo lo puede.
Money can do everything.

Con dinero baila el perro, y pan, si se lo dan.
A dog dances with money, and bread, if it's given.

Cuando se va para rico hasta las mulas paren potricos.
When you become rich even the mules bear colts.

El dinero habla.
Money talks.

El dinero lo puede todo.
Money is all powerful.

Con dinero no se olvidan los encargos.
With money commands are not forgotten.

No se cuenta dinero en frente de los pobres.
You don't count money in front of the poor.

Sesos de borrico tiene el que vive pobre para morir rico.
Who lives poor to die rich has the brains of an ass.

Money
Dinero

Salió más caro el caldo que los frijoles.
The soup turned out to be more expensive than the beans.

Por eso se va la moneda, porque siendo redonda, rueda.
That is why money goes—because, being round, it rolls.

Nadie al cielo rico va; todo aquí lo dejará.
No one goes to heaven rich; everything will be left behind.

Al rico no debas y al pobre no prometas.
Never owe a rich person, or make promises to a poor one.

A quien más rico que tú es, ni le quites, ni le des.
*From anyone who is wealthier than you, to give or to
take will not do.*

Aquellos son ricos que tienen amigos.
Wealthy are those that have friends.

El que mucho tiene, mucho se inquieta.
Who has much, worries much.

El rico, como el marrano, no rinde hasta que no muere.
Wealthy people, and pigs, only share once they are dead.

A quien nada quiere, todo le sobra.
To someone who wants nothing, everything is surplus.

En casa de rica, ella manda y ella grita.
In a rich woman's house, her hollers and orders ring out.

*El dinero se paga,
pero el favor no.*

Money can be
repaid, but not
the favor.

Money
Dinero

El dinero en la bolsa, hasta que se gasta no se goza.

Más caga un buey que cien golondrinas.
One ox excretes more than a hundred swallows do.
(*Influential people make a bigger mess.*)

Money is a friend only when you spend.

Aunque seas muy grande y rico, necesitas del pobre y chico.
Though you may be wealthy and tall, you still will need the poor and small.

Cuesta más trabajo guardarlo que ganarlo.
It's more trouble to keep it than to earn it.

Lo barato es caro.
What's cheap is expensive.

Salir en un ojo de la cara.
To cost an eye from my face.
(*To cost an arm and a leg.*)

Más vale bien de lejos que mal de cerca.
Better good things from afar than bad things close up.

Más vale un Judas de oro que un crucifijo de acero.
A gold Judas is worth more than a crucifix of steel.

No hay cosa más barata que la que se compra.
There is nothing cheaper than what one has bought.

Más vale el 50% de algo, que el 100% de nada.
Fifty percent of something is better than 100% of nothing.

Poverty
Pobreza

No hay cosa más mala que para algo no valga.
There is nothing so bad that it isn't good for something.

*Más vale algo
que nada.*

Anything is better
than nothing.

No hay corazón tan triste como una bolsa sin dinero.
You won't find a heart as sad as a pocket without money.

El dinero del pobre, dos veces se gasta.
A poor person's money is twice spent.

Tripa vacía, corazón sin alegría.
Empty belly, unhappy heart.

Algo es algo, peor es nada y algo vale más que nada.
*Something is something, worse is nothing, and something
is worth more than nothing.*

¿Que mayor riqueza, que vivir contento con pobreza?
What better wealth than to live content with poverty?

El hombre necesitado, cada año apedrado.
A needy man is abused year in and year out.

Pobre pero honrado.
Poor but honest.

Pobreza no es deshonra.
Poverty is no dishonor.

Pobreza no es vileza, pero por ahí empieza.
Poverty is not vile, but it starts around there.

Poverty
Pobreza

No todos podemos ser ricos pero podemos ser buenos.

Not all of us can be rich but we can all be good.

Al que no le sobre pan, que no críe perro.
One who has no leftover bread should not raise a dog.

Los pobres son muy liberales de palabra.
The poor are very liberal with words.

Más vale pan con amor que gallina con dolor.
Better bread with love than chicken with grief.

Más vale pan con amor que galleta con dolor.
Better bread with love than cookies with grief.
(Better to be poor and happy than rich and troubled.)

No culpa de gula al que nunca tuvo hartura.
No one is guilty of gluttony who has never had their fill.

La cárcel y la cuaresma, para los pobres están hechas.
Jails and lent were made for the poor.

El que poco tiene, poco teme.
Who has little, worries little.

Cuando el coyote predica, no están seguro los pobres.
When the coyote preaches, the poor are not safe.

Pereza, llave de pobreza.
Laziness: key to poverty.

No tiene cola que le pisen.
Doesn't even have a tail to step on.

Poverty
Pobreza

Dichosos los pobres.
Blessed are the poor.
   —New Testament, Luke VII, 20

Quien vergüenza tiene vive flaco y muere pobre.
One who is always shy will live skinny and die poor.

El que ha de ser medio aunque ande entre tostones.
He was meant to be mediocre, though he goes among fifty-cent pieces.

El que ha de ser pobre, aunque ande entre ricos.
He was meant to be poor, though he mixes with the rich.

El que ha de ser real sencillo, aunque ande entre doblones.
Though he walks with gold coins, he is really a simple coin.

El que ha de ser peso, aunque ande entre los dólares.
He was meant to be a peso, though he walks with dollars.

Sin dinero se sufren las penas más.
Without money sorrows hurt more.

¿Dónde vaya el buey que no are?

Where will a person who doesn't work go?

Security
Seguridad

Grano en grano,
se llena la
gallina el
buche.

Grain by grain,
the hen fills
its beak.

Lo que viene volando, volando se va.
What flies in, flies out.
(*Easy come, easy go.*)

Así como viene se va.
Easy come, easy go.

Ni al jugador des qué juegue, ni al gastador qué gaste.
Neither give a gambler something to play with, nor a
spendthrift something to spend with.

Ganar uno y gastar dos, no tiene perdón de Dios.
By earning one dollar and spending two,
God's forgiveness won't come to you.

El que tiene cuatro y gasta cinco no necesita bolsa.
Whoever has four and spends five needs no purse.

Quien tiene dos y gasta tres, ladrón es.
A person who has two and spends three is sure to be a thief.

Laguna que no tiene desagüe tiene resumidero.
A lake that has no outlet has a drain.

Padre allegador, hijo expendedor.
Frugal father, spendthrift son.

Lo que otro suda, poco dura.
What someone else has sweat for will slip out of your hands.

Security
Seguridad

Guarda los centavos que los pesos llegarán.
Save your pennies and the dollars will come.

Sembrar para coger y coger para sembrar.
Sembrar para cosechar y cosechar para sembrar.
Sow to reap and reap to sow.

Miel en la boca y guarda la bolsa.
Honey in your mouth and save your money.

La fortuna que vino despacio, no se va de prisa.
A fortune that came slowly will not leave in a hurry.

Muchos pocos hacen un mucho.
Many little bits add up to a lot.

Despacio pero seguro.
Slowly but surely.

Dura pero segura.
Tough but safe enough.

Antes de que acabes no te alabes.
You shouldn't begin to shout until the end is all worked out.
(Don't count your chickens before they hatch.)

Bajo la desconfianza vive la seguridad.
Bajo la desconfianza está la seguridad.
Behind mistrust is security.

No hagas lo que no puedas, ni gastes lo que no tengas.

Don't do what you can't do, nor spend what you don't have.

Security
Seguridad

*Camina sin
moneda y vas
seguro a donde
quiera.*

Walk around
without money
and you'll be
safe wherever
you go.

No te sueltes de una rama sin tener otra agarrada.
Don't let go of one branch without grabbing another.

Más vale paso que dure y no trote que canse.
Better a firm step than a trot that tires.

De puerta cerrada huye el diablo.
The devil flees from a closed door.

El poseedor lleva 90 porciento de ganancia.
Possession is nine tenths of the law.

La posesión casi otorga derecho.
Possession almost grants the right.

Lo que es de todos no es de nadie.
What is everybody's is nobody's.

Tanto tienes, tanto vales.
So much you have, so much you're worth.

Debts
Deudas

Ni prestes, ni pidas prestado.
Neither a borrower nor a lender be.
  —Shakespeare, *Hamlet*

Presta dinero a un enemigo y lo ganarás; préstaselo a un
amigo y lo perderás.
*Lend money to an enemy and you will win the enemy over;
lend it to a friend and you will lose the friend.*

Aunque el deudor muera, la deuda se queda.
Though the debtor dies, the debt remains.

El que paga lo que debe, sabe lo que tiene.
Paga lo que debes, sabrás lo que tienes.
Pay what you owe and you will know what you have.

Debo, no niego; pago, no tengo.
I owe, I don't deny it; pay, I don't have it.

Libro prestado, libro perdido.
A book lent is a book lost.

El que nada debe nada teme.
Owe nothing, fear nothing.

Acreedores tienen mejor memoria que los deudores.
Creditors have better memories than debtors.

Después de un servicio, un mal pago.
After a good service, bad payment.

*Lo prometido es
deuda.*

A promise made
is a debt
unpaid.

Debts
Deudas

De las deudas, lo
mejor es no
tenerlas.

The best thing
about debts is
not having
them.

No hay plazo que no llegue, ni deuda que no se pague.
*There is no time limit that doesn't end, nor any debt that
doesn't come in.*

Un bien con un mal se paga.
Goodness is repaid with badness.

Desnuda un santo para vestir a otro.
Undress one saint to dress another.
(Rob Peter to pay Paul.)

Fuiste fiador, será pagador.
You were the bondsman, you'll be the payer.
(Advice against co-signing or offering bond for others.)

Dale lo suyo a su dueño y gozarás de buen sueño.
*Give your master his share to keep and you'll enjoy a good
night's sleep.*

Pagar es corresponder.
To pay is to correspond.
(Money is social exchange.)

El que nada debe, nada teme.
Who doesn't owe, doesn't fear.

ON TIME

A TIEMPO

Cavar un pozo antes de que tenga sed.
Dig your well before you become thirsty.
(Don't wait until it's too late.)

Todo lo eterno es perpetuo,
lo infinito es espacial, no tienen fin.
All that is eternal is perpetual,
what is infinite is spatial,
neither has an end.

Time
Tiempo

El tiempo todo borra.

Time erases everything.

El tiempo perdido no se recobra.
Tiempo ido, nunca más vencido.
Lost time can never be regained.

El tiempo causa olvido.
Time causes forgetfulness.

Tiempo perdido los ángeles lo lloran.
Lost time: Even the angels cry over it.

El tiempo perdido, los santos lo lloran.
Lost time: The saints cry for it.

Quien tiempo tiene y tiempo atiende, tiempo viene
que se arrepiente.
*Who has time and takes too much time, will find time
to regret.*

El tiempo es justiciero y vengador.
Time is just and avenging.

El tiempo desengaña.
Time takes away all doubt.
(Time will tell.)

El tiempo es gran médico.
Time is a great healer.

Tiempo y reflexión matan pasión.
Time and reflection kill passion.

Time
Tiempo

Tiempos hay para comprar y tiempos hay para vender.
There's a time to buy and a time to sell.

El tiempo es dinero.
Time is money.

El tiempo es oro.
Time is gold.

Quien de dos relojes se sirve, no sabe la hora en que vive.
The person with two watches does not know the hour in which he lives.

Hay que darle tiempo al tiempo.
You must give time some time.

Dar tiempo al tiempo es buen advertimiento.
Good advice: Allow time for time.

Ni tiempo ni hora se ata con soga.
Neither time nor hour can be tied down.
(Time waits for no one.)

No hay tiempo como el presente.
There is no time like the present.

¡Qué tiempos! ¡Qué modales!
What times! What mores!
    —Cicero

El tiempo es como el dinero; se gasta solamente una vez.

Time is like money; it's spent only once.

EN POCAS
PALABRAS

145

Time
Tiempo

El tiempo da consejos.

Time gives counsel.

Hay más tiempo que vida.
There is more time than life.

Cuando la de malas llega, la de buenas no dilata.
When the bad time arrives, the good times are never far behind.

No hay dolor que al alma llegue que a los tres días no se quite.
No pain touches the soul that won't go away in three days.

No hay mal que dure cien años, ni cuerpo que lo resista.
There is no ill that lasts a hundred years, nor anyone who can endure it.

Día llegará en que mi gusto se cumplirá.
The day will come when my pleasure will be fulfilled.

El tiempo es buen amigo y sabe desengañar.
Time is a good friend who knows how to disillusion.
(Time helps you see things clearly.)

Lo que al tiempo se deja, al tiempo se queda.
What is left to time, is left for time.

Es lo mismo llegar a tiempo que ser convidado.
It's the same to arrive on time as to be invited.
(Expressed by people who drop in on others at dinner time, a meeting, or a party.)

Perseverance
Perseverancia

La perseverancia toda cosa alcanza.
Perseverance attains all.

Donde hay gana hay maña.
Where there is desire, there is skill.
(*Where there is a will, there is a way.*)

Donde hay voluntad, hay modo.
Where there is a will there is a way.

El que quiere, puede.
Who has the desire, has the ability.

Más hace el que quiere que el que puede.
The one with heart beats the one who's smart.

Sí se puede.
Yes you can.

Alcanza quien no cansa.
Who doesn't tire gets the best.

Dicen que del agua fría nacen los tepocates.
They say tadpoles are born from cold water.
(*Said upon setting out on an impossible task.*)

El que persevera triunfa.
El que persevera alcanza.
Whoever perseveres, triumphs.

*A muele y muele,
ni metate queda.*

Grind and
grind until the
grindstone is
ground.

Patience
Paciencia

Con tiempo y un ganchito, hasta las verdes se alcanzan.

With time and a small hook, you can even reach the green ones.

(Even the impossible can be attained.)

Con paciencia se comió el piojo a la pulga.
With patience, the louse ate the flea.

Roma no se construyó en un día.
Rome wasn't built in a day.
    —Cervantes, *Don Quixote*

Paciencia y barajear.
Patience, and shuffle the cards.

Con paciencia se gana el cielo.
With patience you can win heaven.

Con paciencia se gana la gloria.
With patience you can win glory.

Con paciencia y salivita un elefante se coge a una hormiguita.
With patience and a bit of spit an elephant gets a tiny ant.

Cuando fuiste martillo, no tuviste clemencia; ahora que eres yunque ten paciencia.
When you were a hammer you had no pity; now that you are an anvil, have patience.

Poco a poco hila la vieja el copo.
Little by little, the spinster spins the ball of wool.

Waiting
Esperar

Con paciencia se gana lo imposible.
With patience you can win the impossible.

Un solo golpe no tumba a un roble.
One blow doesn't fell an oak tree.

Lo que se ha de hacer tarde que se haga temprano.
What needs to be done later should be done earlier.
(Never put off until tomorrow what you can do today.)

El día que la rana tenga pelo.
The day the frog has hair.
(Until hell freezes over.)

Esperar el bien de Dios envuelto en una tortilla.
Waiting for God's goodness wrapped up in a tortilla.

Quien de mano ajena espera, mal come y peor cena.
Who waits for a handout eats poorly and dines worse.

Demorar es gastar.
To linger is to spend.

Como el perro del hortelano, que ni come ni deja comer
al amo.
*Like the dog in his kennel, he won't eat and won't let his
master eat.*

*A aquél que
esperar puede,
todo a su tiempo
y voluntad le
viene.*

Everything
willingly comes
to one who
waits.

Waiting
Esperar

De mañana en mañana pierde la oveja la lana.

Day by day, the sheep lose their wool.

Quien espera zapatos del que muera, mucho tiempo durará descalzo.
Who waits for shoes from the dead, will wait a long time barefoot.
(*The wait for an inheritance is endless.*)

Comer y rascar, todo es comenzar.
With eating and scratching, it's all in beginning.

Ni picha, ni quecha, ni deja batear.
He won't pitch, won't catch, and won't let anyone bat.

Tardiness
Tardanza

A todos diles que sí pero no les digas cuando.
Tell everyone "yes," but don't say when.

Quien tarde se levanta, todo el día trota.
Who gets up late is kept on the trot all day.

Cada perro tiene su hueso aunque se levante tarde.
Every dog has its bone, even if it gets up late.

Nunca es tarde si la dicha es buena.
Good news is never late.

Nunca es tarde para reformarse.
It's never too late to mend one's ways.

En la tardanza está el peligro.
There is danger in lateness.

Vale más año tardío que vacío.
Better a late harvest than an empty one.

Más vale horas antes que minutos después.
It is better to be hours ahead of time than minutes late.

Siempre corriendo y tarde llegando.
Always running and getting there late.

*Más vale tarde
que nunca.*

Better late than
never.

Tardiness
Tardanza

*La puntualidad es
la cortesía de reyes
y reinas, deber
de damas y
caballeros
y costumbre
de gente educada.*

Punctuality is the
courtesy of kings
and queens, the
duty of ladies and
gentlemen, and
the custom
of the well
bred.

Más hace una hormiga andando que un buey echado.
A walking ant does more than an ox lying down.

Cuanto más aprisa, menos adelante.
The faster one goes, the slower the progress.
(*Haste makes waste.*)

Va más rápido el que va solo.
He travels faster, who travels alone.

El que mucho corre, pronto para.
Who runs much, stops soon.

El que más corre, menos vuela.
Who runs much, flies little.

Calle pasajera no cría hierbas.
A busy street grows no weeds.
(*Don't let grass grow under your feet.*)

Laziness
Pereza

Brinca el bostezo de boca en boca.
Yawns jump from mouth to mouth.

La pereza es la llave de la pobreza.
Laziness is the key to poverty.

La pereza es la madre de una vida padre.
Laziness is the mother of a good life.

El perezoso siempre es menesteroso.
The lazy are always needy.

La pereza viaja tan lenta, la pobreza no tarda en alcanzarla.
Laziness travels so slowly that poverty soon catches up.

Al flojo, mandarle; y al mezquino, pedirle.
Command the lazy, ask the poor.

No hay vida más cansada que el eterno no hacer nada.
There's nothing more tiring than forever retiring.

Ociosidad, entretenimiento del diablo.
Idleness is the devil's workshop.

Ociosidad con dignidad.
Idleness with dignity.
   —Cicero

La ociosidad es madre de la filosofía.
Idleness is the mother of philosophy.

"¡Andamos arando!" dijo la mosca, sentada en el cuerno del buey.

"We are plowing!" said the fly, sitting on the horns of an ox.

Early Risers
Madrugadores

Aunque madruge el pobre, siempre llega tarde.

Though a poor man may get up early, he is always late.

Más vale a quien Dios ayuda que quien mucho madruga.
Better to have the help of God than to be an early riser.

Al que madruga, Dios lo ayuda.
God helps one who wakes up early.

El que al alba se levanta, tiene su salud y en su trabajo adelanta.
Who rises with the morning star enjoys good health and in work will go far.

El que de mañana se levanta, de cualquier bulto se espanta.
He who rises early in the day, anything can easily frighten away.

El que madruga, come pechuga.
The early riser eats chicken breast.
(First come, first served.)

El que llega primero, muele primero.
Who arrives first, grinds first (corn for tortillas).

Para un madrugador, otro que no duerme.
For every early riser there is one who didn't sleep at all.
(There is always someone with an edge on you.)

Sol que mucho madruga, poco dura.
A sun that rises too early in the day before very long will go away.

Tomorrow
Mañana

Mañana será otro día.
Tomorrow will be another day.

Hoy por mi, mañana por ti.
Today for me, tomorrow for thee.

Vale más hoy que mañana.
Today is worth more than tomorrow.

Mañana es discípulo de hoy.
Tomorrow is today's disciple.

Por lo que hoy tiras, mañana suspiras.
What you dispose of today, tomorrow you will sigh for.

No dejes para mañana lo que puedes hacer hoy.
Don't put off until tomorrow what you can do today.

Siete días tiene la semana, lo que no puedes hacer hoy,
déjalo para mañana.
*Seven days has every week; what you can't do today, till
tomorrow will keep.*

Hoy pa'unos y mañana pa'otros.
Today for some, tomorrow for others.

*Hoy es el mañana
del cual ayer te
preocupabas.*

Today is the
tomorrow you
worried about
yesterday.

Days
Días

Día de mucho,
víspera de nada.

Day of plenty, eve
of nothing.

El lunes ni las gallinas ponen.
Monday not even the hens lay eggs.

En martes, ni te cases, ni te embarques, ni de tu casa
te apartes.
On Tuesdays, neither marry, nor embark, nor from
your home depart.

No es cosa del otro jueves.
It's not something that happened last Thursday.

Sábado glorioso, te lavo, te plancho y te coso.
Glorious Saturday, I will wash for you, iron for you,
and sew for you.

No hay sábado sin sol, ni domingo sin ranchero.
There is no Saturday without sun, nor Sunday without
a ranch hand.

Months
Meses

Enero y febrero, desviejadero.
January and February, take old folks to the mortuary.

El mes de febrero lo inventó un casero, los demás
de a treinta los que pagan la renta.
*The month of February was invented by a landlord,
the rest by those who pay the rent.*

Febrero loco y marzo otro poco.
February is mad, March is worse.

Febrero loco, marzo airoso, abril llovioso, sacan a mayo
floreado y hermoso.
*Crazy February, windy March, rainy April make May
flowery and beautiful.*

Abril lluvioso hace a mayo hermoso.
April showers bring May flowers.

Goza de abril y mayo que tu agosto llegará.
Enjoy April and May for August is coming.
(*Enjoy your youth.*)

*No digas mal
del año hasta
que se ha
pasado.*

Speak no ill of
the year until
it's over.

CHARACTER
& FATE

LA CARACTER
Y EL DESTINO

De músico, poeta, y loco, todos tenemos un poco.
Every person has a bit of musician, madman, and poet.

El poeta nace, no se hace.
Poets are fated, not created.

A lo tuyo, tú; otro como tú, ninguno.
What's yours is yours alone; there's no other like you.

Natural y figura hasta la sepultura.
*Until the day you die you'll be
a natural personality.*

Rico es aquél que se regocija de su suerte.
Rich is the person who is happy with his lot.

Deeds
Hechos

Uno es arquitecto de su propio destino.
One is an architect of his own destiny.

La práctica hace al maestro.
Practice makes a master.

Cada uno es libre de hacer de su trasero un papalote.
Everyone is free to make a kite out of his own behind.

Quien no sabe lo que vale no vale nada.
Who doesn't know how much he's worth isn't worth a thing.

El derecho nace del hecho.
Right is born from the act.

Del decir al hacer, hay mucho que ver.
*From saying something to doing the deed, there is really
a lot to see.*

Lo que se hace de noche, de día aparece.
Lo que de noche se hace, a la mañana aparece.
If at night it's done, it will show up in the sun.

Lo que hecho es, hecho ha de ser por esa vez.
What's done is done.

Lo que has de hacer, no digas cras, pon tu mano y haz.
*In order to do what must get done, just shut your mouth,
roll up your sleeve, and be begun.*

*Por las acciones
se juzgan los
corazones.*

Our hearts are
judged by our
actions.

Deeds
Hechos

Dicho y hecho.

Said and
done.

Al que le duela la muela, que se la saque.
If your tooth hurts, pull it out.
(*Solve your own problems.*)

Si te pica ráscate.
If it itches, scratch it.

Has lo que digo, no lo que yo hago.
Do as I say, not as I do.

Has de hacer, no lo que quieres, sino lo que debes.
Do not what you want to do but what you have to do.

Más vale un hecho que cien palabras.
A deed is worth more than a hundred words.

Es más fácil hacer las cosas bien que explicar por
qué las haces mal.
*It's easier to do things right than to explain why you
didn't do them right.*

Donde no hay voluntad, no hay fuerza.
Where there is no will, there is no force.

El interés tiene pies.
Interest has feet.

Al mal paso, dale prisa.
If it's disagreeable, do it fast.

Valiente de boca, ligero de pies.
Bold mouth, fast feet.

El valiente vive hasta que el cobarde quiere.
The valiant one lives as long as the coward wishes.

Sólo los valientes tienen miedo.
Only the brave have fear.

El hombre a quien muchos temen a muchos ha
de temer.
A man who is feared by many has many to fear.

Más vale decir aquí corrió que aquí murió.
*Better to say "Here he ran away," than "Here he passed
away."*

No hay valiente que llegue a maestro.
The brave person will never be a master.

El valor no necesita anunciarse.
Courage needs no announcement.

Las ratas son las primeras que abandonan el barco.
The rats are the first to jump a sinking ship.

Tener mal tripas.
To have bad tripes.
(*To lack guts.*)

*Los valientes y
el buen vino
duran poco.*

Brave people and
good wine don't
last long.

Courage and Cowardice
Valor y cobardía

A pesar de ser tan pollo, tengo más plumas que un gallo.

Despite being such a chicken, I've got more feathers than a rooster.

Quien oye trueno, no teme al rayo.
Who hears the thunder will not fear the lightning.

Cada quien es dueño de su miedo.
Everyone is owner of their own fears.

Teme al que no te teme.
Fear the man who doesn't fear you.

Antes de la hora, gran denuedo, venidos el punto, mucho miedo.
Before the deed, courage high; then great fear when the time is nigh.

El miedo es como la sangre, por todas las venas corre.
Fear is like blood, it runs through all the veins.

Donde hay miedo, ni vergüenza da.
Where there is fear, there is no embarrassment.

Cuando hay miedo, ni coraje da.
When there is fear, there is no anger.

El miedo no anda en burro.
Fear does not ride on a burro.

Los cobardes mueren cien veces antes de su muerte.
Cowards die many times before their deaths.
    —Shakespeare, *Julius Caesar*, II, 2

Más vale mearse de gusto que mearse de susto.
Better to pee for delight than to pee of fright.

Pones un espantajo y luego te espantas.
You make a scare and scare yourself.

Mal ladra el perro cuando ladra de miedo.
Badly barks the dog when it barks out of fear.

Perro que ladra no muerde.
A dog that barks doesn't bite.

Perro ladrador, poco mordedor.
All bark, no bite.

Bocado sin hueso.
A bite without a bone.

Cargado de fierro, cargado de miedo.
Weighed down with gear—weighed down with fear.

El gato escaldado, hasta del agua fría tiene miedo.
A cautious cat is even afraid of cold water.

Haz más altas cosas que cazar mariposas.
*Do some things more highly prized
than merely chasing butterflies.*

El cobarde de su sombra tiene miedo.
The coward is afraid of his own shadow.

Courage &
Cowardice
*Valor y
cobardía*

*Qué susto llevaron
las gallinas!*

What a scare for
the chickens!

(When someone
gets frightened.)

Honor
Honor

En todas partes se honra a un profeta, menos en su propia tierra y en su propia casa.
A prophet is not without honor, save in his own country, and in his own house.
   —New Testament, Matthew, XIII, 57

Cuando está abierto el cajón, el más honrado es ladrón.
When an open drawer is left, even the most honorable person turns to theft.

A cada persona, tal honor.
To such a person, such an honor.
(*To each his own.*)

Hombre honrado, primero muerto que injuriado.
A man with honor, death before dishonor.

Honor y provecho no caben en el mismo lecho.
Honor and profit don't fit in the same bed.

Entre más honores, más dolores.
The more honors, the more sorrows.

La honradez es la mejor política.
Honor is the best policy.

Caution
Precaución

Lo mejor del valor es la discresión.
The better part of valor is discretion.
　　—Shakespeare, *Henry* IV, I, V, 4

Hay veces que vale más ser gallina que gallo.

There are times when it is better to be a chicken than a rooster.

Vale más perro vivo que león muerto.
A live dog is better than a dead lion.

Después del pisotón, "usted Dispense."
After stepping on me, "Excuse me."
(*Lame excuse after something that could have been avoided.*)

Después de ojo sacado no vale, "¡Santa Lucía!"
After taking out the eye, it's too late to cry, "Santa Lucía!"

Nomás cuando relampagea se acuerdan de Santa Bárbara.
Only when lightning strikes do they remember Santa Barbara.

Si no puedes ser casto, sé cauto.
If you can't be chaste, be careful.

No todo lo que se puede se debe hacer.
Not everything that can be done should be done.

El que tenga cola de paja, que no se acerque a la lumbre.
If you have a straw tail, you shouldn't get near a fire.

Caution
Precaución

*Más vale
prevenir que
luego lamentar.*

It is better
to prevent than
to lament.

Amarrarse las agujetas antes de irse de pico (hocico).
Tie your shoelaces before you fall on your nose.
(*Tie your shoes before you trip.*)

Mientras el discreto piensa, el necio hace la hacienda.
While the discreet person thinks, the fool builds his farm.

Más vale onza de prudencia que una libra de ciencia.
*An ounce of prudence is worth more than a pound of
science.*

A donde no se mete, se asoma.
Where you do not enter, look in.

Prevención es mejor que curación.
Prevention is better than a cure.

Una puntada a tiempo salva a cien.
A stitch in time saves nine.

Persona precavida vale por dos.
A cautious person is worth two people.

Que no sepa tu mano izquierda lo que hace la derecha.
Don't let your left hand know what you right hand is doing.

El que se va prevenido no es abatido.
Whoever goes prepared is not defeated.

Caution
Precaución

Uno en el saco y otro en el sobaco.
One in a sack and the other under the armpit.

Hombre prevenido nunca fue vencido.
A man's who's prepared will always be spared.

No acaricies al gato sin ponerte guantes.
Don't caress the cat without putting on gloves.

Si oyes un mal son, avísale al talón.
When warning bells peal, turn on your heel.
(Get ready to run at a sign of danger.)

La confianza mata al hombre.
Overconfidence kills.

Busca la salida antes de entrar.
Look for the exit before entering.

Jugar con fuego es peligroso juego.
Playing with fire is dangerous play.

Lento pero seguro.

Slowly but surely.

Necessity
Necesidad

Necesidad y oportunidad le dan valor al cobarde.

Necessity and opportunity give the coward courage.

La necesidad aguza el ingenio.
Necessity sharpens ingenuity.

La necesidad es la madre de invención.
Necessity is the mother of invention.

La necesidad carece de ley.
Necessity respects no law.

La necesidad no respeta fronteras.
Necessity respects no borders.

La necesidad tiene cara de hereje.
Necessity has the face of a heretic.

Libre al muerto has de llamar, no al que nace en libertad.
Only the dead may be called truly free, not those born in liberty.

Un "sí" te liga; un "no" te libra.
A "yes" binds you; a "no" frees you.

Aunque la jaula sea de oro, no deja de ser jaula.
Though the cage may be made of gold, that doesn't keep it from being a cage.

Bardas no hacen una prisión, ni barras una jaula.
Stone walls do not make a prison, nor iron bars a cage.
　　—Lovelace, *To Althea from Prison*

Searching
Buscar

El que busca, halla.
He who searches shall find.

Lo hallado no es robado.
What is found is not stolen.

Al bien buscarlo, y al mal, esperarlo.
Look for the good, attend the bad.

No me busquen porque me encuentran.
Don't look for me because you will find me.

No le busques tres pies al gato ni mangas al chaleco.
Don't look for three feet on a cat nor sleeves on a vest.
(Don't look for trouble where there is none.)

El que le busca tres pies al gato, le halla cuatro.
Whoever looks for three paws on a cat discovers that
it has four.
(If you look for trouble you will find it.)

No hay que buscarle mangas al chaleco.
No need to look for arms on a vest.

El perro que no sale no encuentra hueso.
A dog that doesn't go outside finds no bones.

Con probar nada se pierde.
You can't lose anything by trying.

Buscarás y
hallarás.

Seek and you
shall find.

The Way
El camino

*Nave sin
timón pronta
perdición.*

A ship without
a rudder
is soon
lost.

Andas por mal camino.
You are traveling down the wrong road.

No dejes camino por vereda.
Don't leave a road for a path.

El que boca tiene, a Roma llega.
Whoever has a mouth will get to Rome.

Preguntando se llega a Roma.
By asking you will get to Rome.

Todos los caminos llegan a Roma.
All roads lead to Rome.

No hay que enseñarle el camino al que lo tiene andado.
No need to show the road to one who has already walked it.

A la tierra que fueres, haz lo que vieres.
Whatever land you go to, do things as they show you.

El salir de la posada es la mayor jornada.
Leaving the rest stop is the major part of the journey.

Siempre que ve caballo se le antoja viaje.
Every time he sees a horse, he wants to go on a trip.

Unas veces a pie y otras andando.
Sometimes on foot and other times walking.

The Way
El camino

Lo mismo a pie que andando.
The same on foot as walking.

Más vale rodear que rodar.
Better to go circle around than to roll right through.

Ir de romera y volver ramera, le sucede a cualquiera.
To set out a pilgrim and return a whore can happen to anyone.
(It can happen to the best of us.)

Todo cabe en un costal sabiéndolo acomodar.
Everything fits in a sack if you know how to pack.

Andar de la ceca a la meca.
To go from the royal mint to Mecca.
(To go from place to place.)

¿Donde es tu tierra? Donde la pases, no donde naces.
Where is your land? It is where you pass your days, not the place where you were born.

Arrieros somos, en el camino andamos y a cada paso nos encontramos.
Animal drivers are we, on the road we go, and with every step we say "hello."
(Our paths will meet again.)

El viaje más largo empieza con el primer paso.

The longest journey begins with the first step.

Consequences
Consecuencias

*Como siembras,
segarás.*

Quien siembra vientos, cosecha tempestades.
Who sows winds will reap storms.

*Como siembras,
cosecharás.*

Lo que granjea uno, eso tiene.
What one sows, one has.

As you sow, so
shall you
reap.

El que siembra cadillos recoge espinas.
Who sows burrs reaps thorns.

Cada quien tiene lo que se granjea.
Everyone has what he has earned.

Cada mortal lleva una cruz a cuestas.
Each mortal carries his own cross.

Cada quien con su mal.
Everyone bears his own misfortune.

Cada quien se pone la corona que labra.
Everyone wears the crown he makes.

El que la hace, la paga.
You make it, you pay.
(As you sow, so shall you reap.)

De una espina sale una flor.
From a thorn emerges a flower.

No hay rosa sin espina.
There is no rose without a thorn.

No hay anverso sin reverso.
There is no obverse without a reverse.
(*Every coin has two sides.*)

Quien mal anda, mal acaba.
Who lives badly, ends up badly.

Ya escogiste tu camino.
You have picked your road.
(*You made your bed, now lie in it.*)

El que al cielo escupe, a la cara le cae.
Who spits to heaven has it fall on his face.
(*Spitting against the wind.*)

Donde hay yeguas, potros nacen.
Where there are mares, colts are born.

Las gallinas de arriba cagan a las de abajo.
The hens on top shit on the bottom ones.

Donde las dan, las toman.
Where they give, they receive.
(*Expect to pay the consequences.*)

*No hay efecto
sin causa.*

There
is no effect
without
cause.

FORTUNE

LA FORTUNA

Lo que será, será.
Whatever will be, will be.

Lo que hoy se pierde, se gana mañana.
What's lost today is gained tomorrow.

Si no es como queremos, pasamos como podemos.
If it's not the way we like it, we'll take it as it comes.

La sopa cayó en la miel.
The soup fell in the honey.

El que le desea mal a su vecino, el suyo viene en camino.
Who wishes ill on his neighbor will find it returned
further on down the road.

Hay que tomar lo bueno con lo malo.
You have to take the good with the bad.

Ríe y el mundo reirá contigo, llora y llorarás solo.
*Laugh and the world laughs with you, weep and you
weep alone.*
— Ella Wheeler, *Solitude*

El que ríe al último ríe mejor.
He laughs best that laughs last.
— Sir J. Vanburgh, *The Country House*, II, 5

Quien a solas se ríe, de sus maldades se acuerda.
The person who laughs alone is remembering past sins.

La lágrima es hermana de la risa.
A tear is sister to a laugh.

La risa abunda en la boca de los locos.
Laughter abounds in the mouths of fools.

Quien bien te quiere te hará llorar.
One who loves you truly will make you cry.

Algunos hombres lloran para hacerse víctimas.
Some men cry to make themselves victims.

Gato llorón no caza ratón.
A crying cat catches no mice.

Lo que no se gasta en lágrimas se gasta en suspiros.
What is not spent in tears is spent in sighs.

*Que nunca rió se
cuenta de alguno;
que no haya
llorado, de
ninguno.*

Of those
who have never
laughed you will
find some; but
of those who
have never
cried: not
a single
one.

*Quien hoy llora,
mañana
canta.*

Who cries
today, sings
tomorrow.

Los últimos serán los primeros.
The last will be the first.

Cada subida tiene su bajada.
Every rise has its fall.

Cuando mayor es la subida, tanto mayor es la caída.
The greater the climb, the harder the fall.

Hay que conocer al valle, para poder apreciar a la cumbre.
You have to know the valley to appreciate the peak.

El que sube más alto, más grande porrazo se da.
Who climbs the highest has the biggest fall.

Hay tiempos en que el pato nada y tiempos en que ni
agua beba.
*There are times when the duck swims and times when
he doesn't even drink water.*

Cuando un valde sube, otro baja.
When one bucket goes up, another comes down.

Días de unos, vísperas de otros.
Days for some, eves for others.
(Great day for some, the day before a bad one for others.)

No hay camino más seguro que el que acaban de robar.
*There is no safer road than the one where someone
has just been robbed.*

Ir de mal a peor.
Going from bad to worse.

Salir de Guatemala para entrar a "Guatepeor."
To leave "Guate-bad" and arrive at "Guate-worse."

Muerto el perro, se acabó la rabia.
When the dog dies, the rabies are gone.

El mejor nadador se ahoga.
The best of swimmers can drown.

Así en el mundo como en la mar, se ahoga el que no
sabe nadar.
*In the world as in the sea around, if you don't know how
to swim, you'll drown.*

Lo que no pasa en un año, pasa en un rato.
What doesn't happen in a year, happens in an instant.

Lo que no fue en tu año, no fue en tu daño.
*What didn't happen to you in a year was harmless.
(It was your year—nothing else mattered.)*

Con la vara que midas serás medido.
*The stick with which you measure will also be used
on you.*

Del arbol caído, todos quieren hacer leña.
From a fallen tree, everybody gets firewood.

*Cuando más alto
se sube, más fuerte
es la caída.*

The higher you
climb, the harder
you fall.

Change
Cambio

*Tres cosas
cambian la
naturaleza del
hombre: la
mujer, el estudio
y el vino.*

Three things
change the nature
of men: women,
study, and
wine.

Árbol que no frutea, para la chimenea.
A tree that doesn't give fruit is destined for the fireplace.

Tiempo y viento, mujer y fortuna pronto se mudan.
Time and wind, women and fortune, constantly changing.

Pedro Pino fue y Pedro Pino vino.
Pedro Pino left and Pedro Pino returned.
(*No difference.*)

Es de sabios cambiar de opinión.
It is common among the wise to change opinions.

Cambio de pasto engorda la ternera.
A change of pasture fattens the calf.

Cuando se revuelve el agua, cualquier ajolote es bagre.
When the water is muddied, any water dog is a catfish.
(*Social change produces confusion of moral values.*)

En los nidos de antaño no hay pájaros hogaños.
In the nest left from last year, birds are no longer here.
(*Times change.*)

Cuando una rama se seca, otra se está reverdeciendo.
When one branch is dry, another is turning green.

La fruta de madura cae.
From maturity falls the fruit.

Opportunity
Oportunidad

La naturaleza es el mejor médico.
Nature is the best physician.

Los que bailaron en la otra, que se sienten en ésta.
Those who have danced can sit this one out.
(*Give everybody a chance.*)

Donde una puerta se cierra, otra se abre.
Where one door closes, another opens.

Si una puerta se cierra, cien te quedan.
If one door closes, a hundred are left.

La ocasión la pintan calva.
The occasion is painted bald (*with opportunity*).

La oportunidad llama sólo una vez.
Opportunity knocks only once.

Si uno pierde, otro adquiere.
One person's loss is another's gain.

En cama angosta, métete en medio.
In a small bed, get in the middle.
(*Make the best of a bad situation.*)

Fierro caliente, batirlo de repente.
A hot piece of iron must be beaten immediately.
(*Get it while it's hot.*)

Quien bien baila, de boda en boda anda.

One who dances well will go from wedding to wedding.

(A person with talent is always welcome.)

Hope
Esperanza

La esperanza no es pan, pero alimenta.

Hope is not bread, yet it nourishes.

La esperanza no engorda pero mantiene.
Hope doesn't fatten but it nourishes.

La esperanza engorda, pero no mantiene.
Hope fattens but isn't sustaining.

La esperanza es un pan en lontananza.
Hope is bread for the long distance.

Donde hay vida, hay esperanza.
Where there is life, there is hope.

Quien vive de esperanzas, muere de hambre.
Who lives on hope, dies of hunger.

Lo último que muere es la esperanza.
The last thing that dies is hope.

Cuídate de los buenos, que los malos ya están señalados.
Be careful with the good ones; the bad ones are evident.

Más vale una gota de miel que un barril de hiel.
A drop of honey is worth more than a barrel of bile.

Después de la lluvia, sale el sol.
After the rain, the sun comes out.

Mientras hay alma, hay esperanza.
While there is a soul, there is hope.

Luck
Suerte

El que entra ganando, sale respingando.
Who enters winning, leaves unwilling.

Vale más suerte que dinero.
Luck is worth more than money.

Cada quien tiene la suerte que se merece.
Everyone has the luck he deserves.

La suerte está echada.
The die is cast.

Unos nacen con estrella, otros estrellados.
Some are born with a lucky star, others more like a broken star.

Unos nacen de pie y otros de cabeza.
Some are born feet first and others are born headfirst.

La tercera es la vencida.
The third time is the lucky charm.

Lo que te dio la suerte, no lo tengas por fuerte.
What luck has given to you, you shouldn't regard as due you.

La lucha se hace, la suerte es mala.
A struggle is made, luck is bad.

Al saber le llaman suerte.

Wisdom goes by the name of luck.

Success
Éxito

No todos los caídos son vencidos.

Not all the fallen are vanquished.

Ninguno cante victoria aunque en el estribo esté.
Let no one sing victory though he may be in the saddle.

Puedes ser marrano, pero puedes.
You may be a pig, but you can do it.

De un éxito nacen otros éxitos.
Success breeds success.

No hay que llegar primero sino saber llegar.
You don't have to come in first, but know how to come in.

El que adelante no mira, atrás se queda.
Who doesn't look ahead remains behind.

El que anda entre la miel algo se le pega.
If you hang around honey, some of it will stick to you.

Entre más honores, más dolores.
The more honors, the more sorrows.

Cuando estés en la abundancia, acuérdate de la calamidad.
In times of prosperity, remember calamity.

No es tarde el bien como venga.
When or where good things arrive, they are never late.

El que no arriesga no gana.
Nothing ventured, nothing gained.

Fortuna mal adquirida nunca prospera.
Fortune ill-acquired never prospers.

Hoy figura, mañana sepultura.
Today a rave, tomorrow in the grave.

A cada iglesia le llega su fiestecita.
To every church there comes a fiesta.
(*Everything has its time and place.*)

Desgracia de unos, fortuna para otros.
Disaster for some is good luck for others.

Sobre tus riquezas, no tomes consejos de pobres.
When it comes to your fortune, don't take advice from the poor.

Nada puede la fortuna contra el sabio.
Fortune is no match against the wise person.

El que nunca ha tenido y llega a tener, loco se quiere volver.
One who has nothing and all of a sudden acquires something will go almost mad.

Quien la fama ha perdido, está muerto aunque vivo.
One who has lost fame is living dead.

Por el templo del trabajo se entra a la fama.
Through the temple of labor, one can enter into fame.

Fame &
Fortune
*Fama y
fortuna*

*A la fortuna, sólo
una vez se le ven
las orejas.*

Fortune, you see
its ears only
once.

Fame & Fortune
Fama y Fortuna

Unos tienen la fama y otros cardan la lana.

Some get the fame and others card the wool.

(Some do all the work while others get the credit.)

Crear fama y échate a dormir.
Achieve fame and go to sleep.

El que quiera tener fortuna y fama, no le pegue el sol en la cama.
If it's fortune and fame you prize, don't let sunlight hit you before you rise.

Cóbra buena fama y échate a dormir; cobra mala fama y échate a morir.
Acquire good fame and go to bed; acquire bad fame and go to your grave.

Harto bien baila a quien la fortuna suena.
Dancing well to the fortune of others.

En arbol caído todos suben a las ramas.
Everybody climbs atop a fallen tree.
(*The mighty who have fallen inspire contempt.*)

BAD LUCK & TROUBLE

LA ADVERSIDAD

Ninguna nueva, buenas nuevas.
No news, good news.

Las malas nuevas tienen alas.
Bad news has wings.
(Bad news travels fast.)

Las malas noticias siempre son ciertas.
Bad news is always true.

Lo que pasó, pasó.
What happened, happened.

Lo que pasó, voló.
What is past has fled.

En el mejor paño cae la mancha.
Even the best handkerchief stains.

Loss
Perdida

Lo perdido vaya
por Dios.

May what is lost
go at God's
will.

El bien no es conocido hasta que es perdido.
You don't know what you've got till its gone.

Echando a perder se aprende.
Throwing dice and losing is learning.

Si es para escarmentar, perder es ganar.
If it drives the lesson in, to lose is really but to win.

El que pestañea, pierde.
Who blinks, loses.

Hay que aprender a perder, para empezar a jugar.
One must learn to lose in order to begin to play.

Al mejor cazador se le va la liebre.
Even the best hunter loses a rabbit.

De lo perdido, lo que aparezca.
Whatever turns up comes from what was lost.

De que los hay, los hay (la gracia es dar con ellos).
That there are—there are (the trick is to find them).

Lo que no va en lágrimas, va en suspiros.
What doesn't go tearfully goes sighing.

Want
Falta

Cuando el hambre entra por la puerta, el amor huye por
la ventana.
When hunger comes in the door, love goes out the window.

El hambre es cabrón, pero el que la aguanta es más.
Hunger is a son of a bitch, but whoever can stand it is a
bigger son of a bitch.

El hambre despierta el genio.
Hunger awakens your wits.

Hambre y frío entregan la persona al enemigo.
Hunger and cold surrender a person to the enemy.

Las penas con pan saben menos.
Sorrows with bread don't taste as strong.

Hacer la vida pesada.
To make life difficult.

*No sabemos
lo que vale el
agua hasta
que se seca
el pozo.*

We don't know
the value of
water until the
well runs
dry.

Illness
Enfermedad

No siento que mi niño se enfermó, sino lo mañoso que quedó

I'm not as sorry that my child got sick as I am at how spoiled he has gotten.

Cuida de la recaida que es peor que la enfermedad.
Take care of relapses; they are worse than the illness.

Buenos somos cuando nos enfermamos.
We're very good when we get sick.

Enférmate y veras quién te quiere bien y quién te quiere mal.
Get sick to see who loves you well and who wishes you ill.

Lo que el médico yerra, lo cubre la tierra.
The earth buries a doctor's mistakes forever.

Mala yerba nunca muere.
A bad weed never dies.

Hasta lo que no come le hace daño.
Even what he doesn't eat makes him ill.

El tiempo cura al enfermo, no el ungüento que le embarran.
Time, not the ointment he smears, cures the ill person.

No me hechen ungüento que voy de alivio.
Don't put ointment on me, I am getting well.

Para el catarro: jarro,
Pero si es con tos: dos.
*For a cold: a drink,
But if you cough: two.*

Illness
Enfermedad

En el dedo malo son todos los tropezones.
A sore finger or toe gets all the blows.

Enfermo que caga y mea, el diablo que se lo crea.
An ill person who can shit and pee—if he's sick, well, maybe
the devil would agree.

La enfermedad llega a caballo y se va a pie.
An illness arrives on horseback and leaves on foot.

Es peor el remedio que la enfermedad.
The cure is worse than the illness.

Cuéntale tus penas a quien las pueda remediar.
Tell your problems to one who can cure them.

Lo que no se puede remediar se debe aguantar.
What cannot be cured must be endured.

Mal que no tiene remedio, lo mejor es aguantarlo.
An ill that has no cure one must endure.

Si tu mal tiene remedio, ¿pa' que te apuras?
If there is a cure for your illness, why worry?

Cántaro roto, el remedio es comprar otro.
For a broken jug, the cure is to buy another.

Cuando el mal no
tiene curación,
nomás morirse es
remedio.

When an illness
has no cure, dying
is the only
remedy.

Troubles
Males

El que canta, sus
males espanta.

He who sings
gives worries
wings.

El que no tiene dinga, tiene mandinga.
If it's not one thing, it's another.

Los males entran por libras y salen por onzas.
Troubles come by the pound and leave by the ounce.

No hay mal que por bien no venga.
There is no wrong that doesn't bring some right.
(*Every cloud has a silver lining.*)

Cuando llueve y hace viento, quédate adentro.
When it rains and the wind blows, stay inside.
(*Avoid trouble.*)

El pez que busca anzuelo, busca su duelo.
A fish who looks for the hook, is halfway cooked.
(*If you look for trouble, you will find it.*)

Cada mortal lleva una cruz a cuestas.
Each mortal carries his own cross.

Cada quien con su mal.
Everyone has his own misfortune.

Quien mal pasos anda, malos polvos levanta.
Who takes bad steps raises bad dust.

El que está hecho al mal, el bien lo ofende.
Who was made for discomfort will be offended by comfort.

Troubles
Males

Mal no comunicado, no desechado.
Trouble not communicated will not be resolved.

Un mal no viene solo.
Troubles come by the lot.

Bienvenido, mal, si vienes solo.
Bien vengas mal, si vienes solo.
Welcome, trouble, if you come alone.

Un clavo saca otro clavo.
One grief cures another.

Lo malo se presenta a borbotones.
When it rains, it pours.

Las desgracias nunca llegan solas.
Misfortune never comes alone.
(*When sorrows come, they come not single spies,
but batallions.*
    —Shakespeare, *Hamlet,* IV, 5)

Ir por lana y volver trasquilado.
Going for wool and coming back sheared.

*Un mal llama
a otro.*

One trouble calls
to another.

(When it rains,
it pours.)

Sorrows & Pains
Dolores y penas

¿De dónde vendría el consuelo, si no fuera por el duelo?

Where would comfort come from, if it wasn't for the pain?

Lo que Dios da, para bien será.
What God gives must be for the best.

Cuenta tus duelos y deja los ajenos.
Count your sorrows and leave your neighbor's alone.

A río revuleto, ganancia de pescadores.
A churning river is the fisherman's gain.
(Take advantage of a bad situation.)

Las penas no matan, pero rematan.
Grief doesn't kill but it destroys.

Unos vienen a la pena y otros a la pepena.
Some come for the wake, others for the party.

No hay pena que dure veinte años ni pendejo que la aguante.
There is no pain that lasts twenty years nor fool that will endure it.

No hay dolor que al alma no llegue que a los tres días no se quite.
There is no sorrow the soul can't rise from in three days.

No hay bien que dure, ni mal que no se acabe.
There is no good that lasts, nor bad that does not end.

A más vivir, más sufrir.
The more you live, the more you suffer.

No te alegres de mis penas que cuando las mías
sean viejas, las tuyas serán nuevas.
Do not rejoice over my troubles, because when
they get old, yours will be new.

Duele más el cuero que la camisa.
The skin hurts more than the shirt.

Si quieres que otro se ría, cuéntale tus penas a María.
If you want someone else to laugh, tell your sorrows
to María.

La tristeza que más duele es la que tras placer viene.
The pain that hurts most is the one that follows pleasure.

El que nace para triste, aunque le canten canciones.
Some are born to sadness, even though songs are
sung to them.

Estar más triste que el viernes santo.
Being sadder than Holy Friday.

De gota en gota el vaso reboza.
Drop by drop, the cup runneth over.

La última gota derrama la copa.
The last drop overflows the cup.

Quien espera, desespera (y muere desesperado).
He who waits, despairs (and dies of desperation).

Sorrows &
Pains
Dolores y
penas

Lo malo nunca
es lo peor.

The bad
is never the
worst.

(The worst
is yet to
come.)

EN POCAS
PALABRAS

193

Failure & Blame
Fracaso y culpa

Al mejor escribano se le va un borrón.

The best scribe can make a smudge.

Al músico malo hasta las uñas le estorban.
A bad musician even has trouble with his fingernails.
(Some people have all kinds of excuses when asked to do something.)

De que el cuchillo es malo, le hechan la culpa al herrero.
When the knife is bad, blame it on the blacksmith.

Cuando el arriero es malo, le hecha la culpa a los burros.
When the muleteer is bad, he blames the mules.

El mal escribano le echa la culpa a la pluma.
The bad writer blames the pen.

La mala escritora le echa la culpa a la computadora.
The bad writer blames the computer.

El mal escritor le echa la culpa al redactor.
The bad writer blames the editor.

El mal redactor le echa la culpa al editor.
The bad editor blames the publisher.

Resbalada no es caída, pero es cosa parecida.
A slip is not a fall but the difference is small.

Resignation
Resignación

Una pera en un peral, cuando se cae no es pera;
vale más desesperar que esperar y esperar.
A pear on a pear tree, when it does not fall it is not
a pear; it is better to despair that to wait and wait.
(*The Spanish is a play on words:* pera, espera, desespera.)

Más vale estar "bien parado" que "mal sentado."
It is better to be standing well than sitting badly.

Salga pez o salga rana.
Come out fish or frog.
(*Come what may.*)

Espera lo mejor, prepárate para lo peor, acepta sonriente
lo que venga.
Expect the best, prepare for the worst, and accept with a
smile whatever comes.

Agua pasada no mueve molino.
Water that's gone will not turn the mill.
(*What is done cannot be undone.*)

A lo hecho, pecho.
What's done is done; face up to it.

No se puede soplar y sorber al mismo tiempo.
You can't blow and sip at the same time.

Sea por Dios.
May God's will be done.

Unos nacieron
para moler y
otros para ser
molidos.

Some were born
to grind and
others were
born to be
ground.

GOOD & EVIL

EL MAL Y EL BIEN

La constancia hace milagros.
Consistency creates miracles.

La campana no va a misa, pero avisa.
The bell doesn't go to mass, but it advises.
(*Do as I say, not as I do.*)

Según los ojos que tienen, unos ven males y otros ven bienes.
According to one's own eyes, some see evil, some see good.

A mi no me toca un cura ni en miercoles de ceniza.
No priest ever touches me, not even on Ash Wednesday.

Devil
Diablo

Así paga el diablo a quien le sirve.
That's the way the devil pays whoever serves him.
(*That's the thanks I get for helping you.*)

Cuando el diablo se aburre, juega con la cola.
When the devil is bored, he plays with his tail.
(*An idle mind is the devil's playground.*)

De repente ni el diablo la siente.
So sudden that even the devil will not feel it.
(*Surprise is half the battle.*)

El diablo para hacer de las suyas se vale hasta de
las escrituras.
The devil can cite scriptures for his own purpose.

Más sabe el diablo por viejo que por diablo.
The devil knows more from long life than being a devil.

Cuando el diablo se siente impotente, delega a su mujer.
When the devil feels impotent, he delegates his wife.

El diablo no duerme, anda suelto.
The devil never sleeps, he prowls.

El diablo no es tan feo como lo pintan.
The devil is not as ugly as they paint him.

Quien demonios da, diablos recibe.
Whoever gives hell, will receive devils.

*El diablo puede
tentar, pero no
obligar.*

The devil can
tempt, but not
oblige.

Devil
Diablo

De bien intencionados está el infierno.

Hasta el diablo fue un ángel en sus comienzos.
Even the devil was an angel when he began.
(*It is never too late to change.*)

Hell is paved with good intentions.

Haciéndose el milagro aunque lo haga el diablo.
It's a miracle, even if the devil makes it.

Cuando el diablo reza, engañar quiere.
When the devil prays, he wants to deceive.
(*Beware of showy courtesy and craft.*)

Son muchos los diablos y poco el agua bendita.
There's too many devils and too little holy water.
(*Too many people and not enough good things to go around.*)

Detrás de la cruz está el diablo.
Behind the cross is the devil.

El infierno está lleno de buenos propósitos y el cielo de buenas obras.
Hell is filled with good proposals and heaven with good acts.
(*The road to hell is filled with good intentions.*)

Devil
Diablo

La cruz en el pecho y el diablo en el hecho.
A cross on the chest, and the devil in the action.

El rosario al cuello y el diablo en el cuerpo.
Rosary around the neck and the devil in the body.

Carita de santo, los hechos no tanto.
He has the face of a saint, but his actions don't match.

Ira de hermanos, ira de diablos.
Ire of brothers, ire of devils.

Te asustas con la mortaja y te abrazas del muerto.
You get scared with the shroud and embrace the dead.

El que de santo resbala, hasta el infierno no para.
Whoever slips from sainthood, won't stop until they get to hell.

Lo mal ganado se lo lleva el diablo.

What is ill gotten is claimed by the devil.

Vice
Vicio

La prosperidad descubre vicios; y la adversidad, las virtudes.

Prosperity discovers vice; and adversity virtue.

No hay virtud alguna que la pobreza no destruya.
There is not a single virtue that poverty doesn't destroy.

Todas las virtudes están de acuerdo, los vicios se pelean.
All virtues are in agreement, all vices fight each other.

La fruta prohibida es la más apetecida.
Forbidden fruit is the most appreciated.

Lo prohibido es más apetecido.
Forbidden fruit is more appetizing.

Cuerpo de tentación, cara de arrepentimiento.
Body of temptation, face of regret.

El que sirve a dos amos, queda mal con uno.
Who serves two masters, disappoints one of them.

El que sirve a dos amos, no queda bien con ninguno.
Who serves two masters, disappoints both of them.

El que evita la tentación, evita el pecado.
Whoever avoids temptation, avoids the sin.

Resisto todo menos la tentación.
I can resist everything except temptation.

El que quita la ocasión, quita el pecado.
Avoid the occasion of sin and you'll avoid the sin.

Vice
Vicio

Costumbres de mal maestro, sacan hijo siniestro.
A bad master's habits make a sinister son.

Año nuevo y costumbres las mismas.
A new year and the same habits.

El hábito no hace al monje.
The habit does not make a monk.

Al cabo de un año, tiene el mozo las mañas de su amo.
After a year, the servant has the bad habits of the master.

El que malas mañas ha, tarde o nunca las perderá.
Whoever has bad habits, later or never will lose them.

Lo mejor de los dados es no jugarlos.
The best thing about dice is not to play them.

Juego de manos es de villanos.
Game of hands, game of villains.

El vicio es sabotaje contra uno mismo.
Vice is self-inflicted sabotage.

La sangre se hereda y el vicio se pega.
Blood is inherited and vice is contagious.

La ociosidad es la madre de todos los vicios.
Idleness is the mother of all vice.

El perro que come caca, si no la come la huele.

If a dog eats shit, even when it doesn't eat it, it sniffs it.

(Bad habits are hard to break.)

Vice
Vicio

Piensa mal y acertarás mal.

Think evil and you will find your thoughts confirmed.

Puede más el vicio que la razón.
Vice can overcome reason.

Buena es la libertad pero no el libertinaje.
Liberty is good, but not the libertine.

Comer hasta reventar, beber hasta emborracharse, que lo demás es vicio.
Eat till you burst, drink till you're drunk—the rest is vice.

Contra todos vicios, poco dinero.
A cure for all vice — little money.

Todo lo excesivo es vicioso.
Everything excessive is licentious.

No hay peor vicio que el exceso.
There is no worst vice than excess.

Contra el vicio de pedir, hay la virtud de no dar.
Against the vice of asking is the virtue of not giving.

Greed
Avaricia

Ganar mucho y gastar poco, sí es de ávaro, no es de loco.
Earning a lot and spending little is greed but not madness.

Quien mucho abarca, poco aprieta.
Who embraces a lot, squeezes little.
(*Don't bite off more than you can chew.*)

Quien más tiene, más quiere.
The more you have, the more you want.

No tiene nada, quien nada le basta.
A person who is never satisfied has nothing.

Persona que vive pobre para morir rica, no parece humano sino borrico.
A person who lives poor to die rich is less a human than an ass.

El marrano más trompudo se lleva la mejor mazorca.
The pig with the biggest snout takes the best corn cob.

Les dan almohada y piden colchón.
Give them a pillow and they ask for a mattress.

La avaricia rompe el saco.
Avarice tears the bag.

La codicia rompe el saco.
Covetousness tears the bag.

El que mucho abarca, poco aprieta o se le cansan los brazos.

The person who embraces a lot must squeeze lightly or his arms will tire.

Greed
Avaricia

El que todo lo quiere, todo lo pierde.

Whoever wants everything, loses everything.

Les dan la mano y cogen el pie.
Give them a hand and they grab the foot.

No hallarás un avariento que esté tranquilo un momento.
You won't find an avaricious person who can stay calm for even a moment.

No hallarás un avariento que esté tranquilo y contento.
You will never find a miser who is calm and content.

Pedro Gómez tú lo traes y tú lo comes.
Pedro Gómez, you bring it and you eat it.
(*Comment for someone bringing a delicacy home and eating it alone.*)

Te hacen el favor de un abrazo y quieres que te aprieten.
They gave you a hug and you wanted a squeeze.

De milagro te abrazan y quieres que te besen.
It's a miracle they hug you and you want them to give you a kiss.

De ardor mueren los quemados y de frío los encuerados.
Envy kills those burning with desire and the destitute die from the cold.

Hasta los gatos quieren zapatos.
Even the cat wants shoes.
(*When someone doesn't deserve or need something.*)

Envy
Envidia

Después de que una persona hace su marca en el mundo,
llegan otros con un borrador.
*After a person makes his mark in this world, people will
arrive with an eraser.*

Persona celosa de pulga hace oso.
A person jealous of a flea creates a bear.

Si la envidia tiña fuera, que de tiñosos hubiera.
If envy were a rash, how many people would be scratching.

Si los envidiosos volaran, siempre estaría nublado.
If the envious could fly, it would always be cloudy.

Si la envidia fuera tinta, todos tiñerían con ella.
If envy were dye, we would all dye with it.

La envidia agranda al envidiado y achica al envidioso.
Envy makes the envied greater and the envious smaller.

No hay fiera tan furiosa, cual la mujer celosa.
There is no beast more furious than a jealous woman.

Antes envidiado que compadecido.
Vale más causar envidia que lástima.
Better to be envied than pitied.

Bonito es ver llover aunque uno no tenga milpa.
*It is beautiful to see the rainfall even if one doesn't
own a cornfield.*

*La única persona
que vale la pena
envidiar es la
persona sin
envidias.*

The only person
worth envying is
the person
without
envy.

Pride
Orgullo

El burro y el majadero siempre se cuentan primero.

The burro and the fool always count themselves first.

Alábate burro que no hay quien te alabe.
Praise yourself, jackass—there's no one else to praise you.

No saber el alabado y querer rezar el credo.
*Not knowing the hymn of praise and wanting to
sing the creed.*

Estás en todo menos en misa.
You are in everything except mass.

Antes que acabes no te alabes.
Before you finish, don't praise yourself.

El orgullo siempre antecede la caída.
Pride always precedes the fall.

Tras el orgullo viene el fracaso; tras la altanería la caída.
*Pride goeth before destruction and a haughty spirit
before a fall.*
　　—Old Testament, Proverbs, XVI, 18

De esa toga, murió mi gato.
My cat died from that arrogance.

No lo que fuiste sino lo que eres.
Not what you were but what you are.

El cura no se acuerda cuando era sacristán.
*The priest doesn't remember when he was a sacristán.
(Don't forget who you once were.)*

Theft
Hurto

Pobre con puro, ladrón seguro.
A poor man with a cigar: a sure thief.

Preso por mil, preso por mil quinientos.
Jailed for a thousand or for a thousand five hundred.

Pleito entre ladrones y descúbrense los hurtos.
Fight between thieves and the thefts get discovered.

No hay ladrón que no sea desconfiado.
There is no thief who trusts.

No hay ladrón que no sea llorón.
There is no thief that isn't a crybaby.

La ocasión hace al ladrón.
The occasion makes the thief.

Ladrón que roba a ladrón, tiene perdón.
A thief who steals from a thief is pardoned.

Un lobo no muerde a otro.
One wolf [thief] does not bite another.

Largo de uñas.
Long of nails.
(*Description of someone who steals.*)

Más vale pedir que robar.
It is better to ask than to steal.

*Antes que la ley,
nació la trampa;
y antes el ladrón
que la llave
y arca.*

Before the law,
crime was born;
and the thief
was born
before locks
and keys.

Anger
Enfado

*Procuren que el
enojo no les dure
todo el día.*

Be careful not
to allow anger
to stay
throughout
the day.

(Let not the
sun go down
upon thy wrath.
—New Testament,
Ephesians,
IV, 26)

La respuesta amable calma el enojo.
A soft answer turneth away wrath.
> —Old Testament, Proverbs, xv, 1

Si tienes coraje, anda al trabajo para que se te baje.
If you are angry, go to work so you will cool off.

Si estás colérico, cuenta hasta diez.
If you're angry, count to ten.

Hay miradillas que hasta los árboles secan.
There are looks that will even dry trees.

Ojo por ojo y diente por diente.
Eye for an eye and tooth for a tooth.
> —New Testament, Matthew v, 38–39

La mejor venganza es olvidar la injuria.
The best vengeance is to forget the injury.

Quien perdona sin vengarse, queda en riesgo de salvarse.
*Who forgives without vengeance runs the risk of being
saved.*

Perdonar las injurias es la más noble de las venganzas.
To pardon offenses is the most noble vengeance.

Perdonar al malo, es dejar serlo.
*To forgive an evil person is to let him be evil.
(An evil person should be punished.)*

Evils
Males

Un mal no hace bien a nadie.
A wrong does nobody right.
(*Ill blows the wind that profits nobody!*
    —Shakespeare, *Henry* VI, III, 5)

Dos entuertos no hacen un derecho.
Two wrongs do not make a right.

No hay corazón más negro que'l que no sabe agradecer.
There is no heart darker than one that doesn't appreciate.

Mal haya quien mal piense.
Evil to whoever thinks evil.

El que mal hace, bien no espere.
Whoever does evil, do not expect something good.

El que mal piensa, mal hace.
Who thinks evil, does evil.

El que mal vive, el miedo lo sigue.
Who leads an evil life will be followed by fear.

El pecado trae consigo la penitencia.
The sin carries with it its own penance.

La letra con sangre entra.
Letters enter with blood.

*Haz mal, espera
otro tal.*

Do wrong,
expect wrong
in return.

God
Dios

*Dios me libre de los
buenos consejos,
que de los malos
me libro yo.*

God save me from
good advice, for I
will save myself
from the bad
advice.

¡Primero Dios!
God first!

¡Ay Dios!
Oh God!

¡Bendito sea Dios!
Blessed be God!

A quien Dios quiere, le llena la casa de bienes.
Whoever God likes, he will bless.

Dios consiente pero no siempre.
God spoils—but not always.
(God consents—but not always.)

No hay más amigo que Dios ni más pariente que el peso.
*There is no better friend than God nor better relative than
the dollar.*

Quien Dios se la diera, San Pedro se la bendiga.
Whom God favors, Saint Peter blesses.
(Accept things as they are.)

Dios castiga sin palo ni piedra.
God punishes without sticks or stones.

¡A que mi Dios tan charro que ni las espuelas se quita!
*Oh my God, so much of a cowboy that he doesn't even
take off his spurs!*

God
Dios

Ama y serás amado; teme a Dios y serás
honrado.
Love and you shall be loved; fear God and you
shall be honored.

Cosas a Dios dejadas son bien vengadas.
Things left to God are well avenged.
(*Leave revenge to God.*)

Dios aprieta pero no ahorca.
God squeezes but never chokes.

Dios tarda pero no olvida.
God may be late but he will never forget.

No se mueve la hoja sin la voluntad de Dios.
   —Sancho Panza, in *Don Quixote*
The leaf does not move without the will of God.

Dios no cumple antojos ni endereza jorobados.
God does not grant wishes nor does he straighten
hunchbacks.

Cuando Dios da, da a manos llenas.
When God gives, he gives with full hands.
When God gives, he gives to full hands.

Dios da, pero no acarrea.
God gives, but doesn't carry for you.
(*God helps those who help themselves.*)

Todo vale en el
nombre de Dios.

All is valid in
God's name.

(Even the
devil quotes
scripture.)

God
Dios

No quiero que Dios me dé, sino que me ponga donde haya.

I don't want God to give me but just to put me where there is some.

El hombre propone, Dios dispone y el Diablo lo descompone.
Man proposes, God disposes, and the devil decomposes.

Dios habla por el que calla.
God speaks for the one that keeps quiet.

El hombre propone, Dios dispone, viene la mujer y todo lo descompone.
Man proposes, God disposes; then a woman comes along and it all decomposes.

Donde todo falta, Dios asiste.
Where everything is missing, God assists.

El que no conoce a Dios, donde quiera se está hincando.
One who doesn't know God will genuflect everywhere.

El que no habla, Dios no lo oye.
Who does not speak, God does not hear.

Más puede Dios que el Diablo.
God can do more than the devil.
(It is better to deal with honesty than deceit.)

Dios no se queja, más lo suyo no lo deja.
God doesn't complain, but does what is fitting.

Dios es el que sana y el médico se lleva la plata.
God heals and the physician gets the money.

God
Dios

Dios da el frío conforme a la ropa.
God sends cold according to one's clothes.
(*God tempers the wind to the shorn lamb.*)

Cuando Dios amanece, para todos aparece.
When God awakens, He awakens for all.
(*When the sun comes out, it comes out for everyone.*)

A quien Dios quiere bien, la perra le pare puercos.
Whomever God loves, his dog gives birth to pigs.

A Dios rogando y con el mazo dando.
Praise the Lord and pass the ammunition.
(*God helps those that help themselves.*)

Dios ayuda a los ricos, los pobres pueden rogar.
God helps the rich, and the poor can beg.

El molino de Dios muele despacio pero seguro.
God's mill grinds slow but sure.

Cada uno para si y Dios para todos.
Everyone for himself and God for everyone.

Dios pondrá los medios.
God will provide the means.

A quien Dios quiere bien, uvas le da el laurel.
*Whomever God loves well will give him grapes from
the laurel shrub.*

*Dios da y Dios
quita.*

God gives and
God takes
away.

God
Dios

Tiene Dios más que darnos, que nosotros que pedirle.

God has more to give us than we have to ask him.

Ayúdate que Dios te ayudará.
Help yourself and God will help you.
(*God helps those who help themselves.*)

Dios los cría y ellos se juntan.
God creates them and they unite.
(*Birds of a feather flock together.*)

Dios los hace y solitos se juntan.
God creates them and they unite by themselves.

Dios manda el frío, según la ropa.
God sends cold weather according to one's clothing.
(*Everything is relative.*)

Cuando Dios no quiere, santo no puede.
When God doesn't want to, a saint can't help.

El que a Dios busca, Dios halla.
Who seeks God, finds God.

Faith
Fe

Dichosos los que creen sin haber visto.
Blessed are they who have not seen and yet believed.
— New Testament, John xx, 29

Quien cree en todos yerra; y quien cree a ninguno, acierta.
Whoever believes in everyone errs, and whoever believes in
no one is mistaken.

Créense del aire.
Believe in the air.

Ver para creer.
Seeing to believe.

Hasta que no lo veas, no lo creas.
Until you see it, don't believe it.

Santo Tomás, ver y creer.
Saint Thomas, seeing and believing.

Flor marchita y fe perdida, nunca vuelven a la vida.
A withered flower and lost faith never regain life.

De hombre sin fe, no me fiaré.
A man without faith, I will not trust.

La fe mueve
montes.

Faith moves
mountains.

Charity
Caridad

¿Quieres?
se murió porque
¡Toma! le dio
un palo.

"You want
some?" died
because "Here,
have some!"
beat it with
a stick.

Más vale un "toma" que dos "te daré."
Better one "take this" than two "I'll give it to you later."

Conocen a San "Toma" pero a San "Dame" no.
They know Saint Give but not Saint Take.
(For those who know how to take but not how to give.)

Cuando dicen "¡Toma!" hasta el rey se asoma.
When they say, "Take this!" even the king looks into it.

Repartióse la mar e hízose sal.
The sea was distributed and it turned into salt.

Dan más donde conocen menos.
They give more where they know less.

El que reparte, lleva la peor parte.
The one who distributes gets the smallest portion.

El que parte y reparte, lleva la mejor parte.
The one who cuts and distributes takes the best part.

Ni todo dar, ni todo negar.
Do not give all, nor deny all.

Entre más botones, más ojales.
The more buttons, the more buttonholes.

Más da el duro que el desnudo.
A miser gives more than a naked person.

Charity
Caridad

De dineros y bondad, siempre la mitad.

Of money and goodness, always half.

Entre más se empina uno, más se le ven las nalgas.
The more you bend over, the more your butt will show.
(The more you give, the more people will take advantage of you.)

Cuando te hablen de dinero y de bondad, siempre quita la mitad.
When someone talks to you about money and charity, cut it in half.

Ofrecer y no dar, es deber y no pagar.
To offer and not give is to owe and not pay.

Dar por recibir no es dar sino pedir.
To give in order to receive is not to give but to ask for.

Hay más dicha en dar que en recibir.
It is more blessed to give than to receive.
    —New Testament, Acts xx, 35

Para dar y tener, seso es menester.
To give and take, you have to have brains.

Que lindo es vivir para amar; que grande es tener para dar.
How beautiful it is to live and love; how great it is to have and give.

Caridad y de la buena en casa y luego en la ajena.
The best charity begins at home, and then moves on to the neighbors.

Charity
Caridad

*La caridad
encubre
numerosos
pecados.*

Charity
hides a
multitude
of sins.

La caridad, para dar, empieza en el hogar.
Charity begins at home.

A mí me sobra lo que a tí te falta.
I have an over abundance of what you lack.

El que da lo que tiene, a pedir pronto viene.
Who gives what they have soon returns to ask.

El que da lo que tiene, el diablo se ríe de él.
Who gives what they have, the devil laughs at them.

El que da pan al perro ajeno, pierde el pan y pierde
el perro.
Give bread to a strange dog, lose the bread and the dog.

No da el que puede sino el que quiere.
It's not the one who can give but the one who wants to.

Como campana que todos vienen y te tocan.
To be like a bell that everyone comes and rings.

Quien por otro se apura, ni camposanto merece.
Whoever worries for another, doesn't deserve a cemetery.

Al que bien hacen, bien no esperes.
For whom you do good, do not expect good in return.

Haz bien y no mires a quién.
Do good and never notice to whom.

Charity
Caridad

Cada quien tiene su modo de dar chiche.
Everyone has her own way of breastfeeding.

Da y ten, y harás bien.
Give and retain, and you will do all right.

Dar y quitar, pecado mortal.
To give and take back is a mortal sin.

El que da primero, da dos veces.
Who gives first, gives twice.

El que da y quita, con el diablo se desquita.
Who gives and takes away will have to deal with the devil.

Fraile que pide por Dios, pide siempre para dos.
The friar that asks in the name of God asks for two.
(Prayers are said for the soul and for the donor.)

Amagar y no dar es pecado mortal.
To feign and not give is a mortal sin.

Lo dado, hasta los obispos trotan.
What is given, even the bishops come running.

Hacer bien nunca se pierde.
Doing good is never a loss.

Al que le dan que no escoja.
Who is given should not choose.

Al potro y al niño con cariño.

Treat animals
and children
kindly.

Charity
Caridad

Gratitud es la esperanza de futuros favores.

Gratitude is the hope of future favors.

Fraile que pide pan toma carne si se la dan.
A friar who asks for bread will take meat if it is offered to him.

Farol de la calle, oscuridad de su casa.
Candil de la calle, oscuridad de su casa.
Light of the streets, darkness of his house.

Limosneros con garrote.
Beggars with a club.

Pedir limosna para hacer caridad.
Beg in order to do charity.

El perro y el niño donde ven cariño.
The dog and the child, wherever they see kindness.

El que es buen pato, hasta en el aire nada.
A good duck even swims in the air.

Busquen y encontrarán, llamen a la puerta y se les abrirá.
Seek and ye shall find, knock and it shall be opened unto you.
        —New Testament, Matthew, VII, 7

El río pasado, el santo olvidado.
Safely ashore, we pray to the saint no more.

Si quieres aprender a orar, entra en el mar.
If you want to learn how to pray, jump in the sea.

Prayer
Oración

Bien reza pero mal ofrece.
Prays well but offers poorly.

El que mucho reza, presto acaba.
Who prays a lot, soon finishes.

Tempestad ven y no se hincan.
They see a storm and don't kneel.

Una buena acción es la mejor oración.
A good deed is the best prayer.

*No saber
con cuál mano
persignarse.*

Not knowing what
hand to make
the sign of
the cross
with.

Saints
Santos

¿Pa' qué pedirle a
los santos, habi-
endo tan lindo
Dios?

Why ask the
saints when
there is such a
beautiful
God?

Ni tanto que queme al santo ni tanto que no le alumbre.
Not so close with the candle as to burn the saint nor
so far the saint has no light.

Para santo que es la misa, con un repique basta.
For the saint for whom this mass is said, one ring
of the bell is sufficient.

Se dice el santo pero no el milagro.
You name the saint but not the miracle.

Santo que no es visto no es adorado.
Santo no conocido, no adorado.
The saint that hasn't been seen is not adored.

Cuando hay santos nuevos, los viejos no hacen milagros.
With new saints, the old ones don't work miracles.

La vela se le enciende al santo que se la merece.
The candle is lit to the saint that deserves it.

Río cruzado, santo olvidado.
River crossed, saint forgotten.

Pasado el tranco, el santo olvidado.
Past the distance (sorrow), the saint is forgotten.

A buen santo te encomiendas.
A "good saint" you entrust yourself to.
(Used sarcastically against an untrustworthy person.)

Conscience
Conciencia

Busca tus mejores bienes, que dentro de ti los tienes.
Look for your best virtues; you have them within you.

Virtud es su misma recompensa.
Virtue is its own reward.

Pagan justos por pecadores.
The innocent often pay for the sins of others.

La ropa limpia no necesita jabón.
Clean clothes need no soap.

Cuida más tu conciencia que tu inteligencia.
Take more care of your conscience than your intelligence.

Más vale vergüenza en cara que mancilla en el corazón.
Better shame on your face than stain in your heart.

Quien no tiene vergüenza, toda la calle es suya.
One who has no shame will have the street all to himself.

Más vale una colorada que cien descoloridas.
Better to bear a red face of shame than a hundred discolored faces.

Desde que inventaron los pretextos no se cometen faltas.
Since excuses were invented there have been no more mistakes.

Tu conciencia es testigo, juez y jurado.

Your conscience is witness, judge, and jury.

WISDOM & FOLLY

LA SABIDURÍA
Y LA TONTERÍA

Quien quiere contentar a cada uno, no contentará a ninguno.
Who tries to please all will please no one.

La imitación es el mejor halago.
Imitation is the most sincere form of flattery.

Echando en saco roto.
Putting in a torn sack.
(Sowing in earth that will not produce.)

Apagar el fuego con aceite.
Extinguishing the fire with oil.

Foolishness
Tontos, necios, pendejos y locura

Qué tontos somos los mortales.
What fools we mortals be.
—Shakespeare, *A Midsummer Night's Dream,* III, 2

Si todo el mundo te llama asno, deberás rebuznar.

Los pendejos y la mala suerte siempre van juntos.
Fools and bad luck always go together.

If everybody calls you an ass, they must have heard you braying.

Perritos abren sus ojos a los quince dias, pendejos jamás.
Puppies open their eyes in fifteen days, fools never do.

Cada segundo nace un pendejo.
A fool is born every second.
(*A sucker is born every minute.*)

Para pendejo no se estudia.
You don't have to study to be a fool.

El que es pendejo, no de Dios goza.
A fool doesn't even appreciate God.

Si cada pendejo trajera palo, faltaría leña.
If every fool carried a stick, firewood would be scarce.

Más puede preguntar un necio que responder un cuerdo.
A fool can ask as easily as a normal person can respond.

Se desboca como mula sin mecate.
Running off at the mouth like a mule without a tether.

Foolishness

*Entre
bobos anda
el juego.*

Between fools
goes the
game.

Montan el burro para preguntar por él.
Mount a donkey to ask where he is.
(Ask a dumb question and you get a dumb answer.)

Quien nace para burro, rebuznando muere.
Who was born to be a jackass will die braying.

Este mundo es un fandango, y el que no lo baila
es un asno.
*This world is a big dancing party and whoever
doesn't dance is a jackass.*

Entre mula y mula, nomás las patadas se oyen.
Between jackasses, the only thing you hear are the kicks.

El que nace para buey, del cielo le caen los cuernos.
Born to be an ox, the horns will fall from heaven.

El que nace pa' tamal, del cielo le caen las hojas.
*If you were born to be a tamale, corn husks will fall
from heaven.*
(Born to lose.)

No hay milpa sin huitlacoche.
There is no cornfield without blight.
(There's a fool in every crowd.)

Más sabe el tonto preguntar que cien hombres contestar.
*The fool has more questions to ask than a hundred men
can answer.*

Foolishness

Tontos, necios, pendejos y locura

Haste el tonto y come con las dos manos.
Act like a fool and eat with both hands.
(Do not worry about what the rest of the world thinks.)

El que es tonto, toca el acordeón, come mucho pan
y escribe buena letra.
The fool plays the accordion, eats a lot of bread,
and writes well.
(Said of someone who thinks he knows everything.)

El burro que pateó el panal y se quedó parado.
The jackass that kicked the hive and just stood there.

Mal de muchos, consuelo de tontos.
Ill for many, comfort for fools.

Largo de cabello, corto de seso.
Long of hair, short of brains.

No hay tonto que un viejo tonto.
There's no fool like an old fool.

Hacer caso a pendejos es enaltecerlos.
Pay attention to a fool and you praise them.

Reconocer a pendejos es admitir mucho.
To recognize a fool is to admit a lot.

Hay que tratar exageradamente amable a los pendejos.
You have to be extremely amiable to fools.

Con pendejos ni bañarse porque pierden el jabón.

Never bathe with fools because they will lose the soap.

Foolishness

Con tarugo ni a misa porque se voltea pa'l coro.

Don't even go to mass with a fool because he will face the choir.

Los cortos y los pendejos se conocen desde lejos.
The meek and the fools can be spotted from afar.

Los necios admiran lo que no comprenden.
The obstinate admire what they don't understand.

El bobo si es callado, por sesudo es reputado.
An idiot, if he is silent, has the reputation of being brainy.

Cada chango con su mecate.
Every little monkey with his own leash.

A palabras necias, oídos sordos.
Foolish words, deaf ears.

El sordo no oye pero compone.
The deaf do not hear but they make up their own stories.

¡Que mañana hay misa para los sordos!
There's mass for the deaf tomorrow!
(*Comment for someone who can't or won't hear.*)

No hay peor sordo que el que no quiere oir.
The deafest person is the one who doesn't want to hear.

Entra por aquí y sale por allá.
In one ear and out the other.

Un loco hace cien.
One crazy person makes a hundred.

Foolishness
Tontos, necios, pendejos y locura

Dios me libra de una persona de un libro.
May God save me from a person who knows but one book.
(*Limited knowledge is a dangerous thing.*)

Si los locos usaran coronas, todos seríamos reyes.
If crazies were to use crowns, we would all be kings.

No seas mono porque te bailarán.
Don't be a monkey, because they will dance you.

Cara de bobo, cabeza de lobo,
Face of an fool, head of a wolf.

El ignorante es poco tolerante.
An ignorant person is not very tolerant.

Razones convencen a sabios y a necios los palos.
The wise are convinced by reason, fools by a paddle.

De lo que no sabes, ni censures ni alabes.
Of what you don't know, neither censure nor praise.

La ignorancia no es pretexto.
Ignorance is no pretext.

La ignorancia no quita pecado.
Ignorance doesn't take away the sin.

La ignorancia es madre de la admiración.
Ignorance is the mother of admiration.

*Cada loco con
su tema.*

Each fanatic
with his
fancy.

Foolishness

Tontos, necios, pendejos y locura

Tiene grillos en la cabeza.

He has crickets in the head.

(He's gone bananas, lost his marbles, flipped his lid.)

Sólo sé que no sé nada.
I only know that I know nothing.
  —Socrates

Ignorar es más que errar.
Ignorance is worse than erring.

Quien ignora, ni peca ni merece.
One who ignores, neither sins nor wins merit.

El precio de tu sombrero no corresponde a la medida de tu cerebro.
The price of your hat doesn't correspond with the size of your brain.

Al loco y al aire, se les da la calle.
The crazy, like the wind, are given the right of way.

Todos tienen sombrero, pero no todos tienen cabeza donde ponerlo.
Everyone has a hat but not everyone has a head to put it on.

Como el gallo enano, brinca y no alcanza y así se la pasa el año.
Like a dwarf rooster, he jumps and jumps without reaching, and so he passes the year.

Blindness & Seeing
Ceguera y ver

Si hubiera sido víbora, te pica.
Had it been a snake, it would have bitten you.

En el reino de los ciegos, el tuerto es rey.
In the land of the blind, the one-eyed man is king.

El ciego guiando otro ciego.
The blind leading the blind.

La zorra nunca se ve la cola.
The fox never sees her tail.

A malos ojos no hay cosa buena.
To bad eyes, nothing looks good.

Ojos que no ven, corazón que no siente.
Eyes that can't see, heart that can't feel.

Ver es creer.
To see is to believe.

El que más mira, menos ve.
Who sees much, sees little.
(Seeing the forest but not the tree.)

Los árboles no dejan ver el bosque.
The trees don't allow us to see the forest.

El bosque no deja ver los árboles.
The forest doesn't allow us to see the trees.

No hay peor ciego que el que no quiere ver.

There is no blinder person than the one who does not want to see.

Eyes
Ojos

Más vale ver la paja en el ojo ajeno y no la viga en el propio.

It is better to see the straw in another's eye and not the roof beam in your own.

Ojos que no ven tienen menos que sentir.
Eyes that do not see feel even less.

Donde pone el ojo, pone la bala.
Wherever the eye is aimed, the bullet is aimed.

Lo que veo con los ojos con el dedo lo señalo.
What I see with my eyes I point to with my finger.

Limpia el ojo solo con el codo.
Clean your eye but only with your elbow.

Ojo pendiente, no miente.
An alert eye does not lie.

Ojo que no mira no antoja.
Eye that does not see does not desire.

Por los ojos entran los antojos.
Whims and desires enter through the eyes.

Ojos cerrados no indican ceguera.
Closed eyes don't indicate blindness.

¡Ojos que te vieron ir!
Eyes that saw you leave!

¡Dichosos son mis ojos!
Joyous are my eyes!
(Greeting upon seeing a long lost friend or loved one.)

Face
Cara

Cara de ángel y entrañas de demonio.
Face of an angel and guts of a demon.

Cara de beato, uñas de gato.
Face of a devout person, claws of a cat.

Caras vemos, corazones no sabemos.
Faces we see, hearts we don't know about.

Al mal tiempo, buena cara.
For bad times, put on a good face.

No te cortes la nariz por culpa de tu cara.
Don't cut your nose in spite of your face.

El mal y el bien en la cara se ven.
Good and evil are reflected on one's face.

Amor y dinero a la cara salen.
Love and money reflect in the face.

Como su cara, sus hechos.
Like the face, like the actions.
(A face betrays.)

La cara es el espejo del alma.
The face mirrors the soul.

Sale a la cara, lo contento, lo enfermo y la vergüenza.
Happiness, illness, and shame come forth on the face.

El bien gozado o el mal sufrido, siempre en la cara, nunca escondido.

The happy one and the victim— always in the face, never hidden.

Appearances
Apariencias

*Como te ven, así
te tratan.*

*Como te ven,
te tratan.*

As they see you,
so shall they
treat you.

En este mundo traidor, nada es verdad ni mentira; todo es
según el color del cristal con que se mira.
*In this traitorous world, nothing is true or false; everything
is according to the crystal through which you see it.*

Todo es según el color del cristal por donde se mira.
Everything is colored by the glass you see it through.

En cojera de perro y en lágrimas de mujer, no
hay que creer.
*Never trust a lame dog or the tears of a woman.
(Distrust an exaggerated display of emotions.)*

No todos los que montan a caballo son caballeros.
*Not all who mount a horse are horsemen
(gentlemen, or cavaliers).*

Quien nunca se ríe es gato y quien sempre lo hace
un mentecato.
*The person who never laughs is a cat and the one
who always laughs is an idiot.*

Es la misma gata, nomás un poco revolcada.
It's the same cat, only a little trampled.

No hagas cosas buenas que parezcan malas, ni
malas que parezcan buenas.
*Don't do good things that seem bad, nor bad things
that seem good.*

Appearances
Apariencias

Plato ajeno, parece lleno.
Your neighbor's plate always seems fuller.

Freno dorado no apura al caballo.
A golden bit doesn't hurry the horse.

Las apariencias engañan.
Appearances betray.

No basta ser bueno sino parecerlo.
It is not enough to be good; one must also appear to be good.

No todo lo que brilla es oro.
Not everything that shines is gold.

Aunque la mona se vista de seda, mona se queda.
Although the monkey may dress in silk, she stays a monkey.

Cada cubeta huele a lo que carga dentro.
Each pail smells like what it carries inside.

Ninguno diga quien es, que sus obras lo dirán.
No one say who he is, his deeds will speak for him.

Cada cual es hijo de sus obras.
The work is father to the man.

Mucho ruido y pocas nueces.
A lot of noise but few nuts.

*Junto a lo bueno
está lo mejor.*

Next to the good
is the best.

(The grass is
always greener
on the other
side.)

Appearances
Apariencias

Buenos y tontos se
confunden al
pronto.

Initially it's
hard to tell the
difference
between a good
person and
a fool.

Estar más corrido que escaso.
Being more rundown than rare.

Estar fuera de órbita.
Being out of orbit.

Sentirse como la divina garza.
Feeling like the divine swan.

Estar más tocada que "Las Mañanitas."
More played than "Happy Birthday" [shopworn].

Estudiar para papa y salir camote.
Studying to be a potato and coming out a sweet potato.

Estar de "mírame" y "no me toques."
Being like "look at me" but "don't touch me."

Cada cosa se parece a su dueño.
Everything looks like its owner.
(Outward appearances tell people what you are like.)

Cada quien es como Dios lo hizo.
Everyone is the way God made him or her.

El que es barrigón, aunque lo faje un arriero.
That one will be fat, no matter how much the
muleteer goads him.
(You can't change a person's character.)

Appearances
Apariencias

No hagas cosas buenas que a la vista parezcan malas.
Don't do good things that give the appearance of being bad.

*Con
la intención
basta.*

It's the
intention that
counts.

No todo lo blanco es harina.
Not everything white is flour.

No todo lo de buen aroma es perfume.
Not everything with a good aroma is perfume.

No todo lo que tiene pelo es cepillo.
Not everything that has hair is a brush.

¿Quién te peló que las orejas no te mochó?
Who sheared you and forgot to cut your ears?
(*Comment on short haircuts.*)

Si me quiere con esta cara, si no, vaya.
If you like me with this face, fine, if not, leave.

Hablando del rey de Roma y se asoma.
Speaking of the king of Rome and he shows up.
(*Speaking of the devil.*)

Parecer árbol de Navidad.
Look like a Christmas tree.

Estar de manteles largos.
Dressed in long clothes.

Appearances
Apariencias

*Estar más pando
que un riel curvo.*

Being more
warped than a
curved rail.

Estar de pipa y guante.
Dressed with pipe and glove.

Andar como diablo en panteón.
Walking like a devil in a cemetery.

Andar de Marta la piadosa.
Walking like Martha the pious one.

Andar como alma en pena.
Walking like a wounded soul.

Andar con una mano atrás y otra adelante.
Walking with one hand behind and one hand in front.

Andar más arrancado que las mangas de un chaleco.
Being more torn (excited) than the sleeves of a vest.

Gato encogido, brinco seguro.
A crouched cat is sure to jump.

Donde fuego hace, humo sale.
Where there's smoke, there's fire.

Grande, aunque sea hueso.
Large but all bone.

Clothing
Ropa

En traje de baño no hay engaño.
In a bathing suit, there is no deception.

El traje no hace al hombre pero le da figura.
Clothes do not make the man, but they do give him a figure.

A veces, bajo hábito vil, se esconde hombre gentil.
Rough clothing sometimes conceals a gentle man.

Gato enguantado no pesca ratón.
A gloved cat catches no mice.
(Choose the right clothes or tools for the job.)

Vale más un mal sayo que ir desnudo.
It is better to wear an old garment than to go naked.

El vestido del criado dice quien es el señor.
The appearance of the employee tells you a lot about the boss.

Nadie hay más ingreído que un tonto bien vestido.
There is no one more conceited than a well-dressed fool.

Bien trajado, bien mirado.
Dressed well, looks good.
(Clothes make the person.)

De azul se viste la viuda. / De amarillo la casada.
De blanco la doncella. / De verde la enamorada.
The widow dresses in blue. / In yellow the married woman.
In white the maiden. / In green the one in love.

Al que de ajeno se viste, en la calle lo desnudan.

Whoever dresses in another's clothes may find himself naked in the street.

(False pretensions are soon discovered.)

Shoes
Zapatos

En casa del za-
patero no hay
zapatos.

Zapatos que no hacen ruido, de bandido o de pendejo.
Shoes that make no noise either belong to a bandit or a fool.

In the
shoemaker's
house there are
no shoes.

Saber donde le aprieta el zapato.
Knowing where the shoe pinches.
(Knowing what's best.)

Zapatero a tus zapatos.
Shoemaker, stick to shoes.

Colgar los tenis.
Hang up the tennis shoes.

Irse al cielo con todo y zapatos.
Go to heaven, shoes and all.

Deceptions
Engaños

A otro perro con ese hueso.
Give that bone to another dog.
(*Tell me another one.*)

El que se excusa, se acusa.
Who excuses themselves, accuses themselves.

Quien mucho se excusa, de pecador se acusa.
Whoever excuses themselves too much is sure to be a sinner.

El que engaña con aparencia de verdad es impostor.
Who deceives with an truthful appearance is an impostor.

Quien al Diablo ha de engañar, muy de mañana ha
de madrugar.
Whoever would outwit the Devil must get up very early.

El que solo se engaña, que no se queje.
Whoever deceives himself should not complain.

Engaña a quien te engaña que en este mundo todo
es magaña.
*Deceive the one who deceives you, for everything is
a trick in this world.*

Engañar al engañador no es deshonor.
To deceive the deceiver is not a dishonor.

Cumple con todos y fía de pocos.
Do well by all and trust few.

*No es oro todo lo
que reluce.*

Not everything
that glows is
gold.

Deceptions
Engaños

*A quien de ti
se fía, no lo
engañes.*

Don't
deceive one
who trusts
you.

Si engañas al médico, al confesor o al abogado tú eres
en realidad el engañado.
*If you deceive the doctor, the confessor, or the attorney,
you are in reality the deceived.*

La confianza también mata.
Trust also kills.

En la confianza está el peligro.
In trust is the danger.

El que deja para otro día, de Dios desconfía.
Who leaves something for another day, doesn't trust God.

El método ideal para engañar a la gente es decir la verdad.
The best way to deceive people is to tell them the truth.

En boca de mentiroso, lo cierto se hace dudoso.
In the mouth of a liar, the truth becomes doubtful.

Hacer caravana con sombrero ajeno.
To greet people wearing someone else's hat.
(To take another person's thoughts, opinions, or ideas.)

Fingir no es mentir.
Pretense is not lying.

Lies
Mentiras

Embustero conocido, ya nunca es creído.
Known liars, are no longer credible.

La mentira no tiene pies.
A lie doesn't travel on its own.

Mentira general, pasa por real verdad.
A general lie passes for gospel truth.

Los que dicen mentiras deben siempre tener buena
memoria.
Those who tell lies should always have good memories.

Antes se atrapa al mentiroso que al cojo.
It's easier to catch a liar than a cripple.

La mentira es como el maíz; siempre sale.
The lie is like maize; it always comes out.

La mentira presto es vencida.
The lie is soon found out.

Dura la mentira hasta que llega la verdad.
The lie lasts until the truth arrives.

La trucha y la mentira, mientras más grande, mejor.

With fish and with lies, the bigger, the better.

Experience
Experiencia

No es verlas como experimentarlas.

It is not the same to see them as to experience them.

No vengo a ver si puedo, sino porque puedo vengo.
I don't come to see if I can, but come because I can.

La experiencia lo hace a uno práctico.
Experience makes one practical.

La experiencia es madre de la ciencia.
Experience is the mother of science.

Diligencia es mejor que ciencia.
Diligence is better than science.

Cuando termina la vida de la escuela, comienza la escuela de la vida.
When the life of school ends, the school of life begins.

No hay mejor maestra que la necesidad y pobreza.
There is no better teacher than necessity and poverty.

Lo que bien se aprende nunca se olvida.
What you learn well you never forget.

Lo que bien se aprende, tarde se olvida.
What is well learned is not soon forgotten.

Más enseña la adversidad que diez años de universidad.
Adversity teaches more than do ten years of university.

Al que no ha usado huaraches, las correas le sacan sangre.
Whoever has not worn sandals will bleed from the straps.

Education
Enseñanza

Uno viste al santo para que otro lo baile.
One dresses the saints so that others can dance with them.
(*Once you teach them the trade, they are on their own.*)

Dime lo que lees y te diré lo que crees.
Tell me what you read and I'll tell you what you believe in.

Libro cerrado no hace letrado.
A closed book does not make a literate person.
(*A closed book teaches no one.*)

No hay libro tan malo que no tenga algo bueno.
There is no book so bad that it has no good.

Escarmentar en cabeza ajena.
To learn from another's mistake.

El alfabetismo es enemigo de la esclavitud.
Literacy is the enemy of slavery.

Hay quien sólo sabe leer en su propio libro.
There are those who only know how to read their own book.

Lo que se aprende en la cuna, siempre dura.
What is learned in the cradle lasts forever.

Los necios y los porfiados hacen ricos a los letrados.
The foolish and the stubborn make the learned ones wealthy.

Amarga es la raíz del estudio, pero muy dulce su fruta.

Study is a bitter root, but how sweet is the fruit.

Education
Enseñanza

Saber es poder.

Knowledge is
power.

Enseñando se aprende.
You learn by teaching.

Aprender a gatear antes de caminar.
Learn to catwalk (crawl) before walking.

Quien habla dos lenguas vale por dos.
One who speaks two languages is worth two people.

Me extraña que siendo araña no sepas como tejer.
*It surprises me that being a spider you don't know how to
spin a web.*

El que mucho duerme, poco aprende.
Sleep much, learn little.

Cuando más se estudia, tanto más se sabe.
Cuanto menos se estudia, tanto menos se sabe.
Cuanto más se sabe, tanto más se olvida,
Cuanto más se olvida, tanto menos se sabe,
Entonces, ¿por qué estudiar?
The more you study, the more you know.
The less you study, the less you know.
The more you know, the more you forget.
The more you forget, the less you know,
So why study?

Cada maestrito tiene su librito.
Every little master has his own little favorite book.

Education
Enseñanza

El que luce entre las ollas no luce entre las señoras.
Whoever shines among the pots and pans does not shine among ladies.
(*Education and training will make an impression on women.*)

Aprende cada día cosas que no sabías.
Every day, learn things you did not know.

Quien más sabe, mayores dudas tiene.
The more you know, the greater the doubts.

No hay mejor escuela que la que el tiempo da.

There is no better school than that of time.

Knowledge
Conocimiento

Entre tesoro escondido y oculta sapiencia, no se conoce alguna diferencia.

Between hidden treasure and hidden knowledge, there is no known difference.

El saber no ocupa lugar.
Knowledge occupies no certain place.

Quien se cree de más saber, más tiene de que aprender.
The know-it-all has the most to learn.

Más vale saber mucho de algo que poco de todo.
Better to know a lot of something than a little of everything.

Sufre por saber y trabaja por tener.
Suffer for knowledge and work for wealth.

Más vale saber que tener.
Knowledge is worth more than wealth.

Cada quien sabe lo que carga en su costal.
Everyone knows what he carries in his sack.

Oír, ver y leer aumenta el saber.
Listening, looking, and reading increase knowledge.

La verdad es hija de Dios.
Truth is the daughter of God.

La verdad es hija de Dios y heredera de su gloria.
Truth is the daughter of God and heir to His glory.

Burla, burlando, verdades soltando.
Tease, teasing, truth goes fleeing.

Realidades son verdades y no esperanzas falsas.
Realities are truths and not false hopes.

La verdad no peca pero incomoda.
Truth does not sin but it can make you uncomfortable.
(Truth does not sin, but it can cause a lot of trouble.)

Si dices la verdad no pecas, pero no sabes los males
que suscitas.
You do not sin if you tell the truth, but you don't know
the troubles you cause.

Los borrachos y los niños siempre dicen la verdad.
Drunks and children always tell the truth.

Los niños y los locos dicen las verdades.
Children and madmen tell truths.

La verdad es amarga.
The truth is bitter.

Truth
Verdad

La verdad
huye de los
rincones.

Truth avoids
corners.

Truth
Verdad

La verdad, aunque amarga, se traga.

Truth, no matter how bitter, is swallowed.

La verdad, aunque severa, es amiga verdadera.
The truth, no matter how severe, is a truthful friend.

La verdad, como el aceite, siempre queda encima.
Truth, like oil, always stays on top.

La verdad no se viste de muchos colores.
Truth does not dress up in many colors.

Más verdades se han de saber que decir.
More truths should be known than said.

Quien mucho jura, poca verdad dice.
Whoever swears much, offers little truth.

La verdad sale como el maíz.
The truth rises like maize.

La verdad padece pero no perece.
Truth suffers but never dies.

Todo saldrá en la lavada.
Everything will come out in the wash.

La mentira es hija del diablo; la verdad es hija de Dios.
The lie is the devil's daughter; truth is God's daughter.

El bobo si es callado, por sesudo es reputado.
Even a fool, when he holds his peace, is counted wise.
—Old Testament, Proverbs, XVII, 28

*La sabiduría es
más preciosa que
las perlas.*

Wisdom is rarer
than rubies.

Cuando el sabio yerra, el necio se alegra.
When the wise person errs, the fool rejoices.

La misa, dígala el cura.
Mass, let the priest say it.
(*Leave some things to the experts.*)

Reflexión es la madre de la sabiduría.
Reflection is the mother of wisdom.

Siempre sigue consejos de los sabios y los viejos.
Always follow the advice of the wise and the old.

Es de sabios cambiar de opinión.
A sign of the wise to change opinion.

Oír, ver y callar es la conducta del sabio.
To listen, look, and remain silent is the conduct of a sage.

Nada cuesta soñar.
It costs nothing to dream.

Los sueños, sueños son.
Dreams are only dreams.

Farewells
Despedidas

El que mucho se despide, pocas ganas tiene de irse.
Who bids good-bye many times has little desire to go.

El que se va para la villa, pierde su silla.
Whoever goes to the village loses his seat.

El que se va para Sevilla, pierde su silla.
Whoever goes to Seville loses his seat.

Lo mismo es irse, que juirse que irse sin licencia.
*It's all the same whether you leave in flight or simply
without permission.*

Piedra que rueda no crea moho.
A rolling stone gathers no moss.

¡A Dios y vámonos!
God's will—and away we go!

*El que no crea en
despedidas, que se
despida.*

One who
doesn't believe in
farewells must
bid farewell.

Bibliography
Bibliografía

Amaro, Juan. *American/Mexican Folk Wisdom in Spanish & English*. Kerrville, Texas: Warm Days of Retirement, nd.

Aranda, Charles. *Dichos: Proverbs and Sayings from the Spanish*. Santa Fe: Sunstone Press, 1977.

Aroroa, Shirley L. *Proverbial Comparisons and Related Expressions in Spanish*. In *Folklore Studies* 29, Los Angeles: University of California Press, 1977.

Ballesteros, Octavio A. *Mexican Proverbs: The Philosophy, Wisdom and Humor of a People*. Austin, Texas: Eakin Press, 1979.

Chalot, Mauricio (Rutilio Camacho Arias). *Dichos y añejires de México*. Mexico City: Edición del autor, 1977.

Coca, Benjamín. *Book of Proverbs*. Montezuma, New Mexico: Montezuma Press, 1983.

Del Pueblo, Juan. *Dichos mexicanos*. Mexico City: Editorial Albatros, nd.

Fernández Bustamante, Adolfo. *Mexicanismos y dichos mexicanos, Todo*. (From *Dichos y refranes de la picardía mexicana* bibliography by A. Jiménez.)

Gallegos Gallegos, Federico. *Antología de proverbios españoles y mexicanos* (thesis). Mexico City: Universidad Nacional Autónoma, Facultad de Filosofía y Letras, 1956.

Glazer, Mark. *A Dictionary of Mexican American Proverbs*. New York: Greenwood Press, 1987.

Gómez Maganda, Alejandro. *¡Como dice el dicho! (Refranes y dichos mexicanos)*. Mexico City: Talleres Litográficos E.C.O., 1963.

Gonzalez Gutierrez, José Trinidad. *Dichos y dicharachos*. Guadalajara, Jalisco, Mexico: Quick Print, 1992.

Bibliography
Bibliografía

Iribarren, José María. *El porqué de lo dichos.* Madrid: Aguilar, 1956.

Islas Escárcega, Leovigildo. *Refranero mexicano.* (From *Dichos y refranes de la picardía mexicana* bibliography by A. Jiménez.) Mexico City: nd., approximately 1958.

Islas Escárcega, Leovigildo y García-Bravo y Olivera, Rodolfo. *Diccionario y refranero charro.* Mexico City: Ediciones Charras, 1969.

Jiménez, A. *Nueva picardía mexicana* (15th edition). Mexico City: Editores Mexicanos Unidos, 1981.

———. *Picardía mexicana* (70th edition). Mexico City: Costa-Amic Editores, 1981.

Marín Saunders, Cesar. *Dichos y hechos de la política peruana: una descripción auténtica, sobría y condensada de los dos procesos electorales y las dos juntas militares.* Lima, Perú: Cesar Martin, Peruvian politics and government, 1963.

Martínez Perez, José. *Dichos, dicharachos y refranes mexicanos.* Mexico City: Editores Mexicanos Unidos, 1981.

Recio Flores, Sergio. *Diccionario comparado de refranes y modismos Español-English.* Mexico City: Editorial Libros de México, 1968.

Rubio, Darío. *Refranes, proverbios y dichos y dicharachos mexicanos* (2nd edition). Mexico City: Editorial A.P. Márquez, 1940.

Rublúo Islas, Luis. *Sahagún y los refranes de los antiguos mexicanos.* Mexico City: Dirección General de Prensa, Memorias Bibliotecas y Publicaciones de la Secretaría de Hacienda y Crédito Público, 1966.

Bibliography
Bibliografía

Sahagun, Bernardino De. *Historia general de las cosas de Nueva España,* chapter 41, "De algunos adagios que esta gente mexicana usaba." Mexico City: Alejandro Valdez, 1829.

Saporta y Beja, Enrique. *Refranero sefardi.* Madrid: Consejo Superior de Investigasiones Cinetíficas, Instituto Arias Montano, 1957.

Torres, Hermenegildo L. *Clasificaciones para miembros de la PUP (Por la Unificación de los Pendejos).* Monterrey, Mexico: 1959.

——. *Cien nuevas clasificaciones para socios de la PUP,* Monterrey, 1971.

Velasco Valdés, Miguel. *Refranero popular mexicano* (9th edition). Mexico City: Costa-Amic Editores, 1980.

Index
Indice

Because many dichos fit into many categories, this index cannot be complete. It indicates some of the pages where readers might begin to discover Latino wit and wisdom on various subjects.

Index
Indice

Index
Indice

Index
Indice

Index
Indice

Index
Indice

Index
Indice

Index
Indice

Index
Indice

© *Cynthia Farah*

The Author
El autor

José Antonio
Burciaga,
1940–1996

JOSÉ ANTONIO BURCIAGA (1940–1996) was born in El Paso and taught at Stanford. He was a co-founder of the Latino comedy troupe Culture Clash, a Chicano activist, an award-winning poet and lecturer, and an accomplished muralist. His writing explores the pain, humor, and joy of Chicanismo. His previous books include *Drink Cultura: Chicanismo, Spilling the Beans: Lotería Chicano,* and *Undocumented Love.* He was a literature winner of the Hispanic Heritage Awards and a winner of the Before Columbus Foundation's American Book Award.

Tony Burciaga died of cancer as the book was being prepared to go to press. In the year that we worked with him, he became a friend to everyone at Mercury House, and we miss him.